DOVER
CHILDREN'S THRIFT CLASSICS

Tarzan

EDGAR RICE BURROUGHS

Adapted by Bob Blaisdell
Illustrated by John Green

DOVER PUBLICATIONS, INC.
Mineola, New York

DOVER CHILDREN'S THRIFT CLASSICS
GENERAL EDITOR: STANLEY APPELBAUM
EDITOR OF THIS VOLUME: ADAM H. FROST

Copyright

Published in Canada by General Publishing Company, Ltd., 30 Lesmill Road, Don Mills, Toronto, Ontario.

Bibliographical Note

This Dover edition, first published in 1997, is a new abridgment of a standard text of *Tarzan of the Apes,* which was originally published by A. C. McClurg & Co., Chicago, in 1914. The introductory Note and the illustrations were prepared specially for this edition.

Library of Congress Cataloging-in-Publication Data

Burroughs, Edgar Rice, 1875–1950.
Tarzan / Edgar Rice Burroughs ; abridged by Bob Blaisdell ; illustrated by John Green.
p. cm. — (Dover children's thrift classics)
Abridgment of: Tarzan of the apes.
Summary: A baby boy, left alone in the African jungle after the deaths of his parents, Lord and Lady Greystoke, is adopted by an ape, whose own infant has died, and raised to manhood without ever seeing another human being.
ISBN 0-486-29530-3 (pbk.)
1. Tarzan (Fictitious character)—Juvenile fiction. [1. Feral children—Fiction. 2. Apes—Fiction. 3. Africa—Fiction. 4. Jungles—Fiction.] I. Blaisdell, Robert. II. Green, John, 1948– ill. III. Title. IV. Series.
PZ7.B9453Tam 1997
[Fic]—dc21
96-49011
CIP
AC

Manufactured in the United States of America
Dover Publications, Inc., 31 East 2nd Street, Mineola, N.Y. 11501

Note

EDGAR RICE BURROUGHS (1875–1950) led a rich and varied life, of which his career as an author was but one part. He served in the U.S. Cavalry until it was discovered that he was underage; once discharged, Burroughs went on to work as a cowboy, gold miner, storekeeper, railway detective and newspaper correspondent. Deciding that he could improve upon the popular dime novel, Burroughs turned to writing fiction, eventually creating westerns, science fiction and popular stories for newspapers and magazines as well as for books, and becoming a millionaire in the process. He was a prolific writer and was able to compose a full-length novel in a weekend, as he proved once on a bet.

Tarzan of the Apes (from which this abridgment was taken) was originally published in 1914, the first in a long and highly successful series centered around that character. Through these books and their many adaptations, Tarzan and Jane have become deeply ensconced in the public imagination, and this retelling of Burroughs' classic retains all the adventure and suspense of their original story in a way that is sure to enthrall young readers.

Contents

CHAPTER	PAGE
1. Out to Sea	1
2. Into the Jungle	8
3. The Apes	14
4. The Light of Knowledge	25
5. "King of the Apes"	35
6. The Strangers	40
7. Burials	49
8. The Call of the Wild	58
9. French Lessons	68
10. Tarzan to the Rescue	84

1. Out to Sea

I HAD this story from one who had no business to tell it to me. I do not say the story is true, for I did not witness it, but my own belief is that it *may* be true. If you do not find it believable, you will at least agree that it is remarkable and interesting.

From the records of the Colonial Office and from a dead man's diary, we learn that a certain young English nobleman, whom we shall call John Clayton, Lord Greystoke, was sent to investigate the conditions in a British colony on the west coast of Africa, whose natives another European country was recruiting as soldiers to use in the collection of rubber and ivory from the tribes along the Congo and Aruwimi rivers.

John Clayton was a strong man—mentally, morally and physically. He was above average height; his eyes were gray, his features regular and strong. He was still young when he was entrusted with this important mission in the service of the Queen, a reward for his past good services. This would be a stepping stone to posts of greater importance and responsibility, he knew; on the other hand, he had been married to Alice Rutherford for scarcely three months, and the thought of taking this fair young girl into the dangers of tropical Africa dismayed him.

For her sake he would have refused the appointment, but she would not have it so. Instead she insisted that he accept and, indeed, take her with him.

On a bright May morning in 1888, Lord and Lady Greystoke sailed from Dover for Africa. A month later they arrived at Freetown, where they chartered a small sailing ship, the *Fuwalda*, which was to bear them to their destination. And here Lord and Lady Greystoke vanished from the sight of the world.

Two months after the Greystokes left Freetown, a half dozen British warships were scouring the south Atlantic for trace of them or their ship, and it was almost immediately that the wreckage of the *Fuwalda* was found upon the shores of St. Helena.

The officers of the *Fuwalda* were bullies, hated by and hating their crew. The captain was a brute in his treatment of his men. So it was that, from the second day out from Freetown, Lord Greystoke and his young wife witnessed harrowing scenes upon the deck of the *Fuwalda*. It was on the morning of the second day, while two sailors were washing down the decks, that the captain stopped to speak with Lord and Lady Greystoke.

The sailors were working backwards toward the little group, who faced away from them. Closer and closer the sailors came, until one of them was directly behind the captain. At that instant the officer turned to leave his noble passengers, and, as he did so, he tripped against the sailor and fell sprawling upon the deck.

His face red with rage, the captain got to his feet, and with a mighty blow knocked down the sailor, who was small and rather old.

The other seaman, however, was a huge bear of a man, with a fierce, dark moustache, and a great bull neck set between massive shoulders. As he saw his mate go down he crouched, and, with a snarl, sprang upon the captain, crushing him to his knees.

Without getting up, the officer whipped a revolver

With a snarl, the seaman sprang upon the captain.

from his pocket and fired point-blank at the great-muscled man before him. But, quick as he was, Lord Greystoke was almost as quick, striking the captain's arm, so that the bullet which was aimed at the sailor's heart struck him instead in the leg.

The captain was angry with Lord Greystoke, but turned on his heel and walked away.

The two sailors picked themselves up, the older man helping his wounded mate to rise. The big fellow, who was known as Black Michael, turned to Clayton with a word of thanks. He then limped off toward the sailors' quarters.

A few days later, at midafternoon, the little old sailor whom the captain had knocked down came along deck to where Lord and Lady Greystoke were watching the ocean. While he polished the ship's brass, he edged close to Lord Greystoke and said, in an undertone, "There's trouble to come, sir, on this here ship, and mark my word for it, sir. Big trouble."

"What do you mean, my good fellow?" asked Lord Greystoke.

"Why, hasn't you seen what's goin' on? Hasn't you heard that devilish captain and his mates has been knockin' the bloomin' lights out of half the crew? Black Michael's as good as new again, and he's not going to stand for it; mark my word for it, sir."

"You mean, my man, that the crew is thinking of mutiny?"

"Mutiny!" exclaimed the old fellow. "Mutiny! They means murder, sir!"

"When?"

"It's comin', sir, but I'm not a-sayin' when, and I've said too much now, but you was a good sort the other day, and I thought it right to warn you. So when you hear shootin', git below and stay there." And the old fellow went on with his polishing, which carried him away from where the Greystokes were standing.

"What are we to do, John?" asked his wife. "I shall not urge you to go to the captain. Possibly our best chance lies in keeping a neutral position. If the officers are able to prevent a mutiny, we have nothing to fear, while if the mutineers are victorious, our one slim hope lies in not having tried to stop them."

"Right you are, Alice. We'll keep to the middle of the road."

The next morning, as Lord Greystoke was coming up on deck for his walk before breakfast, a shot rang out, and then another, and another.

Facing the little group of officers was the entire crew of the *Fuwalda,* and at their head stood Black Michael.

At the first return of shots the men ran for shelter, and then shot again at the five officers. Two of the mutineers had been shot and lay where they had fallen. Soon the first mate, in his turn, was killed, and at the cry of command from Black Michael, the bloodthirsty ruffians charged the remaining four officers.

The captain was reloading his revolver when the charge was made. Both sides were cursing and swearing in a frightful manner, which, together with the gunshots and the screams of the wounded, turned the deck of the *Fuwalda* into a madhouse.

Before the officers had taken a dozen backward steps, the men were upon them. A burly sailor killed the captain with an axe, and an instant later the other officers were down.

Short and grisly was the work of the mutineers, and through it all Lord Greystoke stood aside, puffing on his pipe, as though watching a cricket match. As the last officer went down, Greystoke thought that it was time that he returned to his wife. He feared for her safety. As he turned to descend the ladder, he was surprised to see his wife standing on the steps, almost at his side. "How long have you been here, Alice?"

"Since the beginning," she replied. "How awful, John. Oh, how awful!"

The men had by this time surrounded the dead and wounded officers, and began throwing both living and dead over the sides of the vessel. One of the crew spied the Lord and Lady Greystoke, and with a cry of: "Here's two more for the fishes," rushed toward them with an uplifted axe.

But Black Michael was even quicker, so that the fellow went down with a bullet in his back before he had taken a half dozen steps. With a loud roar, Black Michael pointed to Lord and Lady Greystoke, and cried: "These here are my friends, and they are to be left

On the fifth day land was sighted by the lookout.

alone. Do you understand? I'm captain of this ship now, and what I says goes!" Turning to Lord Greystoke, he said, "Just keep to yourselves, and nobody'll harm you." And then he looked threateningly on his fellows.

Lord and Lady Greystoke followed Black Michael's instructions, and thereafter saw little of the crew.

On the fifth day following the mutiny, land was sighted by the lookout. Black Michael announced to Lord Greystoke that, if the place was habitable, he and Lady Greystoke were to be put ashore with their belongings.

"You'll be all right there for a few months," he explained, "and by that time we'll have been able to make a coast somewheres and escape a bit. Then I'll see that your government's notified of where you be, and they'll soon send a ship to fetch you off."

Lord Greystoke protested against the inhumanity of landing them upon an unknown shore, to be left to the mercies of savage beasts and, possibly, still more savage men. But his words only angered the new captain, and so Lord Greystoke decided to make the best he could of a bad situation.

Before dark the ship lay peacefully at anchor in the sighted land's harbor. The surrounding shores were beautiful and green, while in the distance the country rose from the ocean in forested hills. No signs of human life were visible, but there was much bird and animal life, and a little river could be seen.

Black Michael told the Greystokes to prepare to land in the morning. "You saved my life once, and in return I'm going to spare yours, but that's all I can do," he said. "The men won't stand for any more, and if we don't get you landed pretty quick they may even change their minds about giving you that. I'll put all your stuff ashore with you. With your guns for protection, you ought to be able to live here easy enough until help comes."

After he had left them, they went to their room below deck, filled with gloomy thoughts. Lord Greystoke thought that if he had been alone, he might hope to survive for years, for he was a strong, athletic man. But what of Alice, and that baby to whom she would soon give birth?

2. Into the Jungle

EARLY THE next morning their numerous chests and boxes were hoisted on deck and lowered to the waiting boats for transportation to shore. Also loaded were salted meats and biscuits, with a small supply of potatoes and beans, matches, cooking pots, a chest of tools and old sails with which to make tents. Black Michael accompanied the Greystokes to shore, and there he wished them good luck.

Later, as the *Fuwalda* passed out of the harbor, Lady Alice threw her arms around her husband's neck and burst into sobs. "Oh, John," she cried, "the horror of it. What are we to do?"

"There is but one thing to do, Alice," he said quietly, "and that is work. Work must be our salvation. Hundreds of thousands of years ago our ancestors faced the same problems we must now face. What did they do that we may not do?"

"I only hope you are right, John. I will do my best to be a brave, primitive woman, a fit mate for a primitive man."

A hundred yards from the beach was a little level spot, fairly free of trees, and here they decided to build a permanent house, although for the time being they both thought it best to construct a little platform in the trees, out of reach of any savage beasts.

Greystoke selected four trees which formed a rectangle about eight feet square, and, cutting long branches from other trees, he constructed a framework around them, about ten feet from the ground. Across this framework Greystoke placed other, smaller branches quite close together. Seven feet higher he constructed a lighter platform to serve as a roof, and from the sides of this he suspended the sailcloth for walls. When it was completed they had a rather snug little nest.

All during the day the forest about them had been filled with chattering monkeys and excited birds with brilliant feathers. That night, the Greystokes had scarcely closed their eyes when the terrifying cry of a panther rang out from the jungle behind them. For an hour or more they heard it sniffing and clawing at the trees which supported their platform, but at last it roamed away across the beach. They slept very little, and they were relieved when they saw the day dawn. As soon as they had made and finished their breakfast, Greystoke began work upon their home, for he realized that they could hope for no safety and no peace of mind until four strong walls barred the jungle life from them.

The task was a hard one and required the better part of a month, though Greystoke built but one small room. He constructed his cabin of small logs, with clay filling in the gaps. At one end he built a fireplace of small stones from the beach. These also he set in clay, and when the house had been entirely completed, he put on a coating of clay over the entire outside. In the window opening he set small branches, and wove them so that they could withstand the strength of a powerful animal. Thus they obtained air and ventilation. The A-shaped roof was thatched with small branches laid close together, and over these long grass and palm fronds, with a final coating of clay.

The door he built of pieces of the packing-boxes

which had held their belongings; he nailed one piece upon another until he had a solid door some three inches thick. After two days' hard work, he carved out two hardwood hinges, and with these he hung the door so that it opened and closed easily.

The building of a bed, chairs, table and shelves was a relatively easy chore, so that by the end of the second month they were well settled, and, but for the constant dread of attack by wild animals, they were not uncomfortable or unhappy. At night great beasts snarled and roared outside their tiny cabin, but they soon paid little attention to them, sleeping soundly the whole night through.

One afternoon, while Greystoke was working upon an addition to their cabin (for he thought about building several more rooms), a number of birds and monkeys came shrieking through the trees from the direction of the ridge.

Approaching through the jungle in a semierect position, now and then placing the backs of its closed fists upon the ground, was a great ape. As it advanced, it growled deeply and made an occasional low barking sound.

Greystoke was at some distance from the cabin, having come to cut down a perfect tree for his building. He had left his rifles and revolvers within the little cabin, and now that he saw the great ape crashing through the underbrush directly toward him, he felt a shiver of fear. He knew that, armed only with an axe, his chances against this monster were small indeed. There was yet a slight chance of reaching the cabin. He turned and ran toward it, shouting an alarm to his wife to run in and close the door.

Lady Greystoke had been sitting a little way from the

Armed only with an axe, his chances were small indeed.

cabin, and when she heard the cry, she looked up to see the ape springing with an almost incredible swiftness in an effort to cut off her husband. Greystoke cried out, "Close and bolt the door, Alice. I can finish this fellow with an axe." But he knew he was facing a horrible death, and so did she.

The ape was a great bull, weighing probably three hundred pounds. His close-set eyes gleamed beneath his shaggy brows, while his great fangs were bared in a snarl as he paused a moment before his prey.

The powerful brute seized the axe from Greystoke's grasp and hurled it away. With another snarl he reached for the throat of Greystoke, but suddenly there was a loud shot and a bullet entered the ape's back between his shoulders.

Throwing Greystoke to the ground, the beast turned upon his new enemy. Screaming with rage and pain, the ape flew at the woman, who immediately fainted.

Greystoke jumped to his feet and rushed forward to drag the ape away from his wife. He pushed him aside easily—for the ape was nearly dead. The bullet had done its work.

Gently, Greystoke lifted his wife's body and bore her to the little cabin, but it was two hours before she came to. When she awoke, her first words were: "O John, it is so good to really be home! I have had an awful dream, dear. I thought we were no longer in London, but in some horrible place where great beasts attacked us."

"There, there, Alice," he said, stroking her forehead, "try to sleep again, and do not worry your head with bad dreams."

That night a little son was born in the tiny cabin beside the forest. Lady Greystoke never recovered from the shock of the great ape's attack, and she was never again outside the cabin, nor did she ever fully realize that she was not in England. In other ways she was quite all right, and she took joy and happiness in her little son.

Lord Greystoke had long since given up any hope of rescue, and so he worked very hard to beautify the interior of the cabin. Skins of lions and panthers covered the floor. Cupboards and bookcases lined the walls. Odd vases made by his own hand from the clay of the jungle held beautiful tropical flowers. Curtains of grass and bamboo covered the windows, and, the most difficult task of all, he had fashioned lumber to neatly seal the walls and ceiling, and had laid a smooth floor within the cabin.

During the year that followed, Greystoke was several times attacked by the great apes which now seemed to continually pass by the neighborhood of the cabin, but he never again went outside without both rifle and revolver. He had been able at first to shoot many of the animals from the cabin windows, but toward the end they learned to fear the strange cabin from where the thunder of death roared.

Greystoke often read aloud to his wife, from the books he had brought for their new home. Among these were many for little children—picture books, first readers—for they had known that their little child would be old enough for these before they might hope to return to England.

The nobleman also wrote in his diary, which he had always kept in French, and in which he recorded the details of their strange life. This book he kept locked in a little metal box.

A year from the day on which her son was born, Lady Alice passed away in the night. Lord Greystoke now had the fearful responsibility of caring for that wee thing, his son, still a nursing babe.

The last entry in his diary was made the morning following her death: "My little son is crying for nourishment—O Alice, Alice, what shall I do?"

And as John Clayton, Lord Greystoke, wrote the last words, he dropped his head upon his arms. His wife lay still and cold in the bed beside him.

For a long time no sound broke the midday stillness of the jungle, save for the pitiful wailing of the tiny baby boy.

3. The Apes

IN THE forest a mile back from the ocean, old Kerchak the Ape was on a rampage. The younger and lighter members of his tribe scampered to the higher branches of the great trees to escape him. The other males scattered in all directions, but not before the brute had attacked and killed one.

Then he spied Kala, who, returning from a search for food with her young babe, did not know he was in such a state of rage. As he turned on her, she made a mad leap into a tree, climbing quickly away. But just as she reached a safe height, her baby lost its hold on her neck and fell to its death on the ground. With a cry of despair, Kala rushed down to its side, but it was too late. With low moans, she sat cuddling the body to her; Kerchak now left her alone. With the death of the infant his fit seemed to have passed.

Kerchak was a huge king ape, weighing perhaps three hundred and fifty pounds. His forehead was low, his eyes bloodshot, small and set close to his flat nose. There was no ape in all the forest that dared to contest his right to rule, nor did the other and larger animals try to bother him.

Old Tantor, the elephant, alone of all the savage beasts, did not fear him—and him alone did Kerchak fear. When Tantor trumpeted, the great ape scurried with his fellows high among the trees.

The tribe of apes over which Kerchak ruled numbered eight families, each family consisting of an adult male and his wives and their young, totaling some sixty or seventy apes. Kala was the youngest wife of a male called Tublat, meaning "broken nose," and the child she had seen dashed to death was her first, for she was but nine or ten years old. She was large and powerful, with a round, high forehead.

When the tribe saw that Kerchak's rage had ceased, they came slowly down from their trees and went back to their business. The young played among the trees and bushes. Some of the adults lay down upon the soft mat of leaves which covered the ground, while others turned over pieces of fallen branches in search of small bugs and reptiles, which formed part of their diet. Others searched the surrounding trees for fruit, nuts, small birds and eggs.

They had passed an hour or so at these activities when Kerchak called them together and, with a word of command to them to follow him, set off toward the sea. They traveled for the most part upon the ground, where it was open, following the paths of elephants, whose comings and goings broke the only roads through those tangled mazes of bushes, vines and trees.

When the apes walked, it was with a rolling motion, placing the knuckles of their closed hands upon the ground and swinging their bodies forward. But when the way was through the lower trees, they moved more swiftly, swinging from branch to branch. And all the way Kala carried her dead baby hugged closely to her breast.

It was shortly after noon when they reached a ridge overlooking the beach. Below them lay the tiny cottage which was Kerchak's goal. He had seen many of his kind go to their death there, killed by the loud noise

The instinct of mother love reached out.

that the white ape's little black stick made—the strange white ape who lived in that wonderful dwelling. Kerchak had made up his mind to own that stick, and to explore the interior of that mysterious den.

Today there was no sign of the man about, and from where they watched they could see that the cabin door was open. Slowly they crept through the jungle toward the little cabin. On, on they came until Kerchak slunk to the door and peered within. Behind him were two males, and then Kala, closely straining the little dead baby to her breast.

Inside the den they saw the strange white ape lying half across a table, his head buried in his arms; on the bed lay a figure covered by a sailcloth, while from the cradle came the wailing of a baby.

Kerchak entered, crouching for the attack, and John Clayton, Lord Greystoke, rose with a sudden start and faced him. But it was too late for him to grab his revolvers from the far wall. Kerchak charged at him and picked him up, crushing the noble Englishman to death.

Kerchak released the man from his arms and turned his attention toward the little cradle, but Kala was there before him. When he would have grasped the child, she snatched it up herself, and she had bolted through the door and into a high tree before he could stop her.

As she took up the little live baby of Alice Clayton, Lady Greystoke, Kala dropped the dead body of her own child into the empty cradle, for the wail of the living had answered the call of motherhood within her.

High up among the branches of a mighty tree, she hugged the shrieking infant to her bosom, and soon the instinct of mother love reached out to the tiny man-child, and he became quiet. Then the son of an English lord and an English lady nursed at the breast of Kala, the ape.

Below her, the beasts within the cabin were examining the contents of the strange dwelling. The rifle hanging upon the wall caught Kerchak's attention; he had yearned for this death-dealing thunderstick for months. He raised a huge hand and tore it from its hook. He began to examine it closely. He peered down the muzzle and fingered every part. During all these investigations the apes who had entered sat huddled near the door, watching their chief, while those outside crowded in the doorway.

Suddenly Kerchak's finger closed upon the trigger. There was a roar in the little room, and the apes fell over one another in their hurry to escape. Kerchak was equally frightened; so frightened, in fact, that he quite forgot to throw aside the gun, and bolted for the door with it tightly clutched in one hand. As he passed through the doorway, the front of the rifle caught upon the edge of the in-swung door so that it closed tightly after the fleeing ape.

When Kerchak came to a halt a short distance from the cabin, he discovered that he still held the rifle and quickly dropped it.

It was an hour before the apes could bring themselves to approach the cabin again, and when they finally did so, they found that the door was closed and so securely fastened that they could not force it open. The cleverly made latch which Clayton had designed for the door had sprung as Kerchak passed through; nor could the apes find a way to get in through the heavily barred windows.

After roaming about the area for a short time, they started back for the deeper forests and the higher land from where they had come.

Kala had not once come to earth with her little adopted baby, but now Kerchak called to her to come along with them, and as there was no note of anger in his voice, she dropped lightly from branch to branch and joined the others on their homeward march. Those of the apes who tried to examine Kala's strange baby were met with bared fangs and low, menacing growls.

It was as though she knew that this baby was frail and delicate and she feared the rough hands of her tribe. Remembering the death of her own little one, she clung desperately with one hand to the new babe whenever they were upon the march.

The other young rode upon their mothers' backs, their little arms tightly clasping the necks, and their legs locked beneath their mothers' arms. Not so with Kala's child; the ape held the small form of the little Lord Greystoke tightly to her breast. She had seen one child fall from her to a terrible death, and she would take no chances with this one.

Tenderly Kala nursed her little orphan, wondering why it did not gain strength as did the little babies of other mothers. It was nearly a year from the time the little fellow came to be her own before he would walk alone, and as for climbing—my, but how stupid he was! He could not even find food alone. Had she known that the child had seen thirteen moons before she had found it, she would have considered it absolutely hopeless, for the little apes in her tribe were as far advanced at two or three moons as was this little stranger after twenty-five.

Tublat, Kala's husband, disliked the newcomer. "He will never be a great ape," he said. "Always you will have to carry him and protect him. What good will he be to the tribe? None; only a burden. Let us leave him quietly sleeping among the tall grasses, that you may bear other and stronger apes to guard us in our old age."

"Never, Broken Nose," replied Kala. "If I must carry him forever, so be it."

And then Tublat went to Kerchak to urge him to force Kala to give up little Tarzan, which was the name they had given to the tiny Lord Greystoke, and which meant "white skin."

But when Kerchak mentioned this to her, Kala threatened to run away from the tribe if they did not leave her in peace with the child. And so he bothered her no more, for the tribe did not wish to lose her.

As Tarzan grew he developed quickly, so that by the time he was ten years old he was an excellent climber, and on the ground could do many wonderful things which were beyond the powers of his little brothers and sisters. In many ways did he differ from them, and they often marveled at his superior cunning, but in strength and size he was lacking, for at ten the great apes were fully grown, some of them over six feet in height, while Tarzan was still but a half-grown boy.

Yet such a boy! From early childhood he had used his hands to swing from branch to branch after the manner of his mother, and as he grew older, he spent hour upon hour speeding through the treetops with his brothers and sisters. He could spring twenty feet across space at the dizzy heights of the forest top, and grasp a wildly waving limb. He could drop twenty feet at a stretch from limb to limb to the ground, or he could swing to the top of the tallest tree with the ease of a squirrel. Though but ten years old, he was fully as strong as the average man of thirty.

His life among these fierce apes was happy, for he did not remember any other kind of life, and he did not know there was any other place than his forest. He was nearly ten before he began to understand that there was a great difference between himself and his fellows. His little body, brown from the sun, suddenly caused him feelings of shame, for he saw that it was entirely hairless, like some snake.

In the higher land his tribe went to a lake, and it was here that Tarzan first saw his face in the clear, still waters. It was on a hot day of the dry season. As he and his cousin leaned over the bank of the lake to drink, both little faces were mirrored in the water. Tarzan was disgusted. It had been bad enough to be hairless, but to have such a face! That tiny slit of a mouth and those puny white teeth! How they looked beside the mighty lips and powerful fangs of his lucky brothers! And the little pinched nose! But when he saw his own eyes, it was frightful. Not even the snakes had such hideous eyes as he.

So taken was he with this horrible sight that he did not hear the stirring of the tall grass behind him; nor did his companion, the ape, for he was drinking. Not thirty paces behind the two, Sabor, the huge lioness, crouched, lashing her tail. Slowly she advanced, her

Behind the two crouched Sabor, lashing her tail.

belly low, almost touching the ground—a great cat preparing to spring upon its prey.

Now she was within ten feet of the two little playfellows—carefully she drew her hind feet up beneath her body. So low was she crouching now that she seemed flattened to the earth. Then, with an awful scream, she sprang.

At that sound, Tarzan leaped into the dreaded water. He could not swim, and the water was very deep. Rapidly he moved his hands and feet, and fell into the stroke called the "dog paddle," so that within a few seconds his nose was above water. He found that he could keep it there by continuing the strokes, and could also make progress through the water.

He was now swimming parallel to the bank, where he saw the cruel beast that would have seized him crouching upon the body of his little playmate. Tarzan raised his voice in the call of distress common to his tribe, adding to it the warning about Sabor.

Almost immediately there came an answer from the distance, and soon forty or fifty apes swung rapidly through the trees toward the scene of tragedy. In the front was Kala, for she had recognized the voice of her beloved.

Though more powerful and a better fighter than the apes, the lioness had no desire to meet these enraged adults, and with a snarl she sprang quickly into the brush and disappeared.

Tarzan now swam to shore. The adventure with the lioness was tragic, but it gave him another new skill, something he, unlike his fellows, continued to pick up through his experiences. Ever after he lost no chance to take a daily plunge in the lake or a stream or the ocean. But for a long time Kala could not get used to the sight of him swimming.

The wanderings of the tribe brought them often near the cabin. Tarzan would peek into the curtained windows, or, climbing upon the roof, peer down the chimney. His childish imagination pictured wonderful creatures within. For hours he would attempt to get in, but he paid little attention to the door, for it seemed just another solid part of the walls.

It was during his next visit to the area near the cabin, following the adventure with old Sabor, that Tarzan noticed that, from a distance, the cabin door appeared to be separate from the wall in which it was set.

The story of his own connection with the cabin had never been told him. The language of the apes had so few words that they could talk but little of what they had seen in the cabin, having no words to describe either the strange people or their belongings. Only in a dim, vague way had Kala explained to Tarzan that his father had been a strange white ape, and he did not know that Kala was not his own mother.

On this day, then, he went to the door and spent hours examining it and fussing with the hinges, the knob and the latch. Finally he stumbled upon the right combination, and the door swung creakingly open. He slowly and cautiously entered.

In the middle of the floor lay a skeleton. Upon the bed lay another, though smaller, while in the tiny cradle nearby was a third, a tiny skeleton. He examined many things—strange tools and weapons, books, papers, clothing. He opened chests and cupboards, and among the other things he found was a hunting knife, on the sharp blade of which he immediately cut his finger. Unfrightened, he continued playing with his new toy.

But then in a cupboard filled with books he came across one with brightly colored pictures—it was a child's illustrated alphabet—

A is for Archer
Who shoots with a bow.
B is for Boy,
His first name is Joe.

The pictures interested him. There were many apes with faces similar to his own, and further along in the book he found, under "M," some little monkeys. But nowhere was pictured any of his own tribe; in all the book was none that looked like Kerchak or Kala.

At first he tried to pick the little pictures from the pages, but he soon saw that they were not real. The boats, trains, cows and horses were meaningless to him, but not quite so strange as the odd little figures which appeared beneath and between the colored pictures—some kind of bug he thought they might be, for many of them had legs, though nowhere could he find one with eyes and a mouth. It was his first introduction to the letters of the alphabet, and he was more than ten years old.

Of course he had never before seen print, and he was quite at a loss to guess the meaning of these strange marks. Near the middle of the book he found his old enemy, Sabor, the lioness, and further on was coiled Histah, the snake.

Oh, it was so interesting! It was approaching dusk when Tarzan put the book back in the cupboard and closed its door, for he did not wish anyone else to find and destroy his treasure. As he went out into the gathering darkness, Tarzan shut the door of the cabin behind him, but not before he had picked up the hunting knife to show to his fellows.

4. The Light of Knowledge

EARLY ONE morning, Tarzan set forth alone to revisit the cabin. It took him only a short time to open again the latch. He then found that he could close and lock the door from within, and this he did so that there would be no chance of his being surprised. He went again to the books. There were some children's readers, picture books and a dictionary. All of these he examined, but the pictures caught his fancy most. Squatting upon his haunches on the tabletop in the cabin—his smooth little body bent over the book, his long black hair falling about his head and over his bright eyes—Tarzan of the Apes was making his way out of ignorance and into the light of learning.

His little face was tense, for he had begun to grasp the solution to the problem of the little marks on the pages. In his hands was a primer opened at a picture of a little ape similar to himself, but covered, except for the hands and face, with strange, colored fur, for such he thought the pants and shirt to be. Beneath the picture were three marks—B-O-Y.

And now he had discovered in the text upon the page that these three marks were repeated many times. Another fact he learned—that there were not very many different marks. Slowly he turned the pages, scanning the pictures and the text for the same series of marks. Soon he found it beneath a picture of another little ape and a strange animal which went upon four

Slowly he turned the pages.

legs like the jackal. Beneath this picture the marks appeared as: A BOY AND HIS DOG.

There they were, the three little marks which always went with the little ape. And so he progressed very, very slowly, for it was a hard task which he unknowingly had set himself—a task which might seem to you or me impossible—learning to read without having the slightest knowledge of letters.

He did not succeed in a day, or in a week, or in a month, or even in a year; but slowly, very slowly, he learned, so that by the time he was fifteen he knew the various combinations of letters which stood for every pictured figure in the little primer and in one or two of the picture books.

One day when he was about twelve, he found a number of pencils in a drawer beneath the table, and, scratching upon the table with one of them, he was delighted to discover the black line it left behind it. He worked so hard with this new toy that the table was soon a mass of scrawly loops and lines. Then he tried to copy some of the little marks that scrambled over the pages of his books. It was difficult, for he held the pencil as one would grasp the hilt of a dagger. But he went on for months, at such times as he was able to come to the cabin, until at last he could roughly copy any of the little marks.

Thus Tarzan made a beginning at writing.

His education progressed; his greatest finds were in the illustrated dictionary, for he learned more through pictures than through words. By the time he was seventeen, he had learned to read the simple child's primer and had realized the true purpose of the little marks.

No longer did he feel shame for his hairless body or his human features, for now his reason told him that he was of a different species from his wild and hairy companions. He was a M-A-N, they were A-P-E-S, and the little apes which scurried through the forest top were M-O-N-K-E-Y-S. He knew, too, that old Sabor was a L-I-O-N-E-S-S, and Histah a S-N-A-K-E, and Tantor an E-L-E-P-H-A-N-T. And so he learned to read.

From then on his progress was rapid.

And soon, his little English heart began to beat with the desire to cover his nakedness with *clothes,* for he had learned from his picture books that all *men* were so covered, while *monkeys* and *apes* and every other living thing went naked.

Many moons ago, when he had been much smaller, he had desired the skin of Sabor, the lioness, or Numa, the lion, or Sheeta, the leopard, to cover his hairless body, that he might no longer look like hideous Histah, the snake. One day, as the tribe continued their slow way through the forest after seeing Sabor, Tarzan's head was filled with his great scheme for slaying his enemy, and for many days he thought of little else. After a terrible rainstorm, in which his tribe was drenched with cold rain, it came to Tarzan that clothes would have kept him warm!

For several months the tribe lingered near the beach where stood Tarzan's cabin, and his studies in the books took up more and more of his time. He did not neglect his body altogether, however; for instance he always, when journeying through the forest, kept a rope ready, with which he practiced until he could throw it as well as a cowboy could a lasso.

Tarzan of the Apes lived on in his wild jungle with little change for several years, except that he grew stronger and wiser, and learned more and more from his books of the strange worlds which lay somewhere outside the forest.

To him, life was never dull. There was always Pisah, the fish, to be caught in the many streams and little lakes, and Sabor, with her ferocious cousins, to keep one ever on the alert. Often they hunted him, and often he hunted them, and though they never quite reached him with those sharp claws, yet there were times when one could scarce have passed a leaf between their talons and his smooth hide. Quick was Sabor, the lioness, and quick were Numa and Sheeta, but Tarzan was lightning.

Only with Tantor, the elephant, did he make friends. On many moonlit nights Tarzan and Tantor walked together, and when the way was clear Tarzan rode, perched high upon Tantor's mighty back. All others in the jungle were his enemies, except his own tribe.

He spent many days during these years in the cabin of his father, where there still lay, untouched, the bones of his parents and the little skeleton of Kala's baby. At eighteen, Tarzan could read and understood nearly everything in the books on the shelves. Also, he could write, with printed letters, but script he had not mastered; he could read it, but with great trouble. Thus, at eighteen, we find him, an English lordling, who could speak no English, and yet who could read and write his native language. Never had he seen a human being other than himself.

High hills shut off the little home of his tribe on three sides, the ocean on the fourth. Though alive with lions and leopards and snakes, the jungle was isolated and undisturbed. But as Tarzan of the Apes sat one day in the cabin reading, the old safety of his jungle was broken forever.

At the far eastern edge, along a hilltop, was a line of fifty warriors, armed with spears and long bows and poisoned arrows. On their backs were oval shields, in their noses huge rings, while on their heads they wore colorful feathers. Across their foreheads were tattooed three lines of color, and on each chest three circles. Their teeth were filed to sharp points.

Following them were several hundred women and children, the women carrying upon their heads cooking pots and ivory. In the rear were a hundred warriors, similar in all respects to the advance guard.

For three days the line of men and their families marched slowly through the heart of this unknown and untracked forest, until finally, early on the fourth day, they came upon a little spot, near the banks of a small river, which seemed less overgrown than any ground they had yet seen. Here they set to work to build a new village, and in a month a great clearing had been made, huts and fences built, plantains, yams and corn planted, and they had taken up their old life in a new home.

Several moons passed by before they ventured far into the territory surrounding their village. But one day, Kulonga, a son of the old king, Mbonga, wandered far into the dense jungle of the west. Carefully he stepped, his spear ever ready, his long oval shield grasped in his left hand close to his body. At his back was his bow, and in the quiver many arrows, well smeared with poison.

Night found Kulonga far from the safety of his village, so he climbed into the fork of a tree and curled himself up to sleep. Three miles to the west of him slept the tribe of Kerchak.

Early the next morning the apes began searching for food. Tarzan made his way to the cabin, picking up his breakfast along the way. The apes scattered by ones, twos and threes in all directions. Kala had moved along an elephant track toward the east, and was busily searching under fallen trees for tasty bugs, when a strange noise caught her attention.

Down the trail, fifty yards away, she saw a strange and fearful creature—Kulonga. Kala turned and went rapidly away along the trail. Close after her came Kulonga. Here was meat! He could make a killing and feast well this day. On he hurried, his spear ready for the throw. At a turning of the trail he cast his spear, and it grazed Kala's side.

With rage and pain, the ape turned upon the man. As she charged, Kulonga shot an arrow at her, and this cut straight into her heart. He heard the other apes approaching, and he turned and ran, fleeing like an antelope.

On the far beach, by the little cabin, Tarzan heard the faint cries and sad moanings of his tribe. He hurried toward the scene, and when he arrived he found the entire tribe gathered jabbering around the dead body of his mother.

Tarzan's grief and anger roared out. He beat upon his chest with his clenched fists, and then he fell upon Kala and sobbed. So what if Kala was a fierce and hairy ape! To Tarzan she had been kind, she had been beautiful. After his grief Tarzan controlled himself, and, questioning the members of the tribe who had witnessed the escape of the murderer, he learned all that their words and signs could tell him.

They told of a strange, hairless ape with feathers growing upon its head, who shot a death-dealing stick from a slim branch, and then ran away. Tarzan now leapt into the trees and swung rapidly through the forest. All day Tarzan followed Kulonga, catching up to him, but not dropping upon him, for the ape-man saw the magical death the warrior was able to produce by flicking the string of his bow and sending a short straight stick into the skin of even a wild boar, not to mention a hyena or a monkey.

Tarzan thought much on this wondrous method of slaying as he swung slowly along at a safe distance behind his enemy. That night Kulonga slept in the fork of a huge tree, and far above him crouched Tarzan of the Apes.

When Kulonga awoke, he found that his bow and arrows had disappeared. The warrior was furious and frightened. He searched the ground below the tree, and he searched the tree, but there was no sign of them. He was defenseless now, except for a knife. His only hope

He took the headdress and placed it on his head.

for life lay in reaching the village as quickly as possible. As soon as he began running, Tarzan swung quietly after him. Kulonga's bow and arrows were tied high in the top of a tree, where Tarzan could find them later.

As Kulonga continued his journey Tarzan traveled almost over the warrior's head. He was anxious to discover where the warrior was going. Just as they came in view of the great clearing where the new village lay, Tarzan dropped his lasso around Kulonga's neck and pulled him to a stop. Tarzan leapt down and plunged his knife into Kulonga's heart.

Kala, Tarzan's foster mother, was avenged.

The ape-man examined the warrior closely, for never had he seen any other human being. The warrior's knife and belt attracted him, and so he took them. A copper anklet also took his fancy, and he took it and put it on his own leg. Finally, he took the feathered headdress and placed it on his own head.

Then he removed his rope from the warrior's neck and dashed up a lofty tree, where he sat on a perch from which he could view the village of thatched huts. Along the tree tops he then made his way for a closer look. He came to rest, finally, in a tree within the village. Below him he observed a new, strange life.

There were naked children running and playing in the village street. There were women grinding dried plantain in stone mortars, while others made little cakes from the flour. Out in the fields he could see still other women gardening. All wore grass skirts, and many were loaded with brass and copper anklets, armlets and bracelets. Tarzan of the Apes looked with wonder at these creatures. He saw several men dozing in the shade, while at the outskirts of the clearing he caught glimpses of armed warriors.

Finally his eyes settled on the woman directly beneath him. Before her was a pot standing over a low fire, and in it bubbled a thick, reddish, tarry substance. On one side of her lay a number of wooden arrows, the points of which she dipped into the liquid, before setting them upon a narrow rack which stood at her other side.

Tarzan knew nothing of poison, but his reasoning told him that it was this liquid on the arrows that killed, and not the arrows themselves. How he should like to have more of those little sticks! If the woman would only leave her work, he could drop down, gather up a handful and be back in the tree again. As he was trying to think of some plan to distract her, he heard a wild cry from across the clearing. A warrior was shouting and waving his spear.

The village was in an uproar instantly. Armed men rushed from their huts and raced toward the warrior. After them trooped the old men, and the women and children too, until, in a moment, the village was deserted.

Quickly Tarzan dropped to the ground beside the pot of poison, gathered up all the arrows he could carry under one arm, and disappeared back up the tree. The sun was high in the heavens. Tarzan had not eaten this day, and it was many miles back to the place where his tribe was gathered. So he turned his back on the village and melted away into the leafy darkness of the forest.

5. "King of the Apes"

THE NEXT day, Tarzan was practicing with his bow and arrows at the first gleam of dawn. Before a month had passed he was a good shot.

The tribe continued to find the hunting good near the beach, and so Tarzan of the Apes varied his archery practice with further reading of his father's books. It was during this period that the young English lord found hidden in the back of the cabin's cupboards a small metal box. In it he found a faded photograph of a smooth-faced young man, a golden locket on a small gold chain, a few letters and a small book.

The photograph he liked most of all, for the eyes of the man were smiling. Though he could not have known, it was of his father. The locket, too, took his fancy, and he placed the chain about his neck in imitation of the men he had seen. The handwritten letters he could hardly read, so he put them back in the box with the photograph and turned his attention to the book. This was filled with handwriting, but while the little marks were all familiar to him, their combinations were strange, and he could not understand them.

It was the diary—kept in French—of John Clayton, Lord Greystoke. Tarzan replaced the box in the cupboard, but always remembered the smiling face in the photograph.

That night he slept in the forest not far from the village, and early the next morning set out slowly on his homeward march, hunting as he traveled. Suddenly he saw Sabor, the lioness, standing in the center of the trail not twenty paces from him. The great yellow eyes were fixed upon him, and the red tongue licked its lips as Sabor crouched, worming her way with belly flattened against the earth.

Tarzan unslung his bow and fitted a poisoned arrow, and as Sabor sprang, he let loose his shot to meet her in midair. At the same instant Tarzan of the Apes jumped to one side; and as the great cat struck the ground beyond him another death-tipped arrow sunk deep into her. With a roar the beast turned and charged once more, only to be met with a third arrow; this time, however, she was too close for the ape-man to avoid, and Tarzan went down beneath the great body of his enemy, his knife drawn and thrust into her. For a moment they lay there, and then Tarzan realized that she was dead.

He got up and placed a foot upon the body of his powerful enemy, and roared out the awful challenge of a victorious ape. The forest echoed with the roar, and birds fell still, and the larger animals and beasts of prey slunk away.

Before Tarzan set out for his tribe he skinned the animal; then he hurried along to show his fellows the trophy. "Look!" he cried. "See what Tarzan, the mighty killer, has done. Who else among you has ever killed one of Numa's people? Tarzan is mightiest amongst you."

These remarks angered Kerchak, and he erupted in a fury, challenging the smooth-skinned ape to fight. The tribe rushed into the trees to avoid the coming violence, and from high above they watched.

Kerchak stood nearly seven feet on his short legs. He

He faced Kerchak now with only his hunting knife.

had enormous shoulders and a snarling face, with fearsome fangs.

Awaiting him stood Tarzan, only six feet in height. His bow and arrows lay some distance away, where he had dropped them while showing Sabor's hide to his fellow apes; he faced Kerchak now with only his hunting knife. As his foe came roaring toward him, he held out his knife and rushed swiftly to meet the attack. Just as their bodies were about to crash together, Tarzan of the Apes grasped one of Kerchak's wrists, and then drove his knife into the chief's body, below the heart.

Kerchak was dead!

Withdrawing the knife, Tarzan placed his foot upon the neck of his enemy, and once again, loud through the forest rang the fierce, wild cry of the winner. And this is how the young Lord Greystoke became King of the Apes.

For a short time the tribe of Tarzan lingered near the beach, for their new chief hated the thought of leaving the little cabin. But when, one day, a member of the tribe discovered great numbers of men from the village clearing a space in the jungle and putting up huts on the banks of the little stream that served as the apes' watering hole, the apes would remain no longer, and so Tarzan led them inland.

Once every moon Tarzan would go swinging back through the branches to have a day with his books, and to replenish his supply of poisoned arrows from the men's village.

The villagers had not as yet discovered Tarzan's cabin on the distant beach, but the ape-man lived in constant dread that, while he was away with the tribe, they would loot his treasures. So it came that he spent more and more time near the cabin, and less and less with the tribe. Soon the apes began to quarrel constantly.

At last some of the older apes spoke to Tarzan on the subject of his frequent absences and the resulting disruptions while he was gone. After giving some thought to the matter, the ape-man told his tribe that he was leaving them. "Tarzan," he explained, "is not an ape. He is not like his people. His ways are not their ways, and so Tarzan is going back to his home by the waters. You must choose another to rule you, for Tarzan will not return."

The following morning, Tarzan set out toward the west and the sea coast. Once there, he decided to steal what few clothes he could from one of the villagers, for nothing seemed to him more of a sign of manhood than clothes and jewelry. He collected various arm and leg bands, and wore them the way he had seen them worn. About his neck hung the golden chain from which hung the locket of his mother. At his back was a quiver of arrows slung from a leather shoulder belt. About his waist was a belt for his knife. Around his waist was a handsome deerskin breechcloth. The long bow which had been Kulonga's hung over his left shoulder.

The young Lord Greystoke, however, worried that he might turn back into an ape, for was not hair beginning to grow on his face? All the apes had hair upon theirs, and so Tarzan was afraid. Almost daily he sharpened his knife and scraped at his young beard.

6. The Strangers

ONE MORNING, from where Tarzan stood by his cabin, a strange sight came to his eyes. On the calm waters of the harbor floated a great ship, and on the beach two small boats were drawn up. A number of white men were moving about between the beach and his cabin. Tarzan saw that in many ways they were like the men in his picture books. He crept closer through the trees until he was quite close to them.

There were many people, unloading boxes and bundles. Tarzan returned to his cabin then, snatched up a piece of paper, and printed on it several lines with a pencil. This notice he stuck upon the cabin door with a splinter. Then, gathering up his precious tin box, his arrows and as many bows and spears as he could carry, he hurried through the door and disappeared into the forest.

Several minutes later, one of the two boats returned to the ship, the *Arrow*, rowed there by burly sailors. Meanwhile, a party of five, including a young, beautiful girl of about nineteen and her heavyset maid, approached the cabin.

One of the five, an older man, a professor, came to the door and read the sign aloud:

THIS IS THE HOUSE OF TARZAN OF THE APES, THE KILLER OF BEASTS AND MANY MEN. DO NOT HARM THE THINGS WHICH ARE TARZAN'S. HE WATCHES.

"Who the devil is Tarzan?" wondered a young man.

"What does 'Tarzan of the Apes' mean?" cried the girl.

"I do not know, Miss Porter," replied the young man. "What do you make of it, Professor Porter?" he added, turning to the old man.

"I have no idea," said the professor.

Two keen eyes had watched every move of the party from behind the leaves of a nearby tree. Tarzan had seen the surprise caused by his notice, and while he could understand nothing of the spoken language of these strange people, their gestures and facial expressions told him much.

After a time, the professor and his assistant, Samuel T. Philander, became interested in the vegetation and wandered off into the jungle, out of sight. Some minutes later, Clayton, the young man, handed the girl his revolver and told her and her maid to go within the cabin and lock themselves in, if possible, while he went and searched for her absentminded father and his assistant.

A few moments later, the maid, Esmeralda, opened the door of the cabin and, entering, let out a shriek of terror.

Jane Porter rushed in and saw the cause of the maid's cry. Upon the floor before them lay the whitened skeleton of a man. A further glance revealed a second skeleton upon the bed.

"What horrible place are we in?" murmured the girl. She crossed the room to look in the little cradle, and saw there a third, smaller skeleton. The girl shuddered, but turned to her shrieking maid and said, "Stop, Esmeralda; stop it this minute! You are only making it worse."

She barred the door from within as Clayton had told

The man leapt upon the lion, choking it with his arm.

her to do, and then she and Esmeralda sat down upon a bench with their arms around one another, and waited.

When Tarzan saw the sailors row away toward the ship, and knew that the girl and her companion were safe in his cabin, he decided to follow the young man into the jungle and learn what his errand might be. He swung off rapidly in the direction taken by Clayton, and in a short time heard in the distance the faint calls of the Englishman to his friends. Tarzan soon caught up to the young man, and he hid himself behind a tree to watch this member of his own species. The fierce jungle would make short work of this stranger if he were not guided in his return to the beach cabin.

Yes; there was Numa, the lion, even now stalking the young man a dozen paces to the right. Clayton heard the great beast nearby, and now there rose the animal's thunderous roar. The man stopped and faced the bushes from which came the awful sound. For a moment all was still. Clayton stood rigid. At last he saw it, not twenty feet away—the long, strong body of a huge, black-maned lion! The beast was upon its belly, moving forward very slowly. Then Clayton heard a noise in the trees above him. There was a twang, and at the same instant an arrow lodged in the yellow hide of the crouching lion.

With lightning speed a man leapt out of the trees upon the lion, choking it with his muscular right arm, while with his left he plunged a knife time and again into the lion's shoulder. In a few moments, the lion sank lifeless to the ground.

Then the strange man, naked except for a loincloth and a few bracelets and necklaces, stood upon the dead body, and, throwing back his head, gave out a fearsome cry.

In the silence that followed the jungle-man's call, Clayton spoke to the man in English, thanking him for his brave rescue, but the only answer was a stare and a shrug. When the bow and quiver had been slung on his back, the wild man once more drew his knife and carved a dozen large strips of meat from the lion. Then, squatting, he began to eat, motioning to Clayton to join him.

But Clayton could not bring himself to share the uncooked meat with his host; instead he watched him, and there dawned upon him the belief that this was Tarzan of the Apes, whose notice he had seen posted upon the cabin door. If so, he must speak English.

Again Clayton tried to speak to the ape-man, but the replies were in a strange language, which resembled the chattering of monkeys and the growling of some wild beast. No, this could not be Tarzan of the Apes, for it was very evident that he did not know English. When the ape-man completed his meal, he rose and, pointing in a different direction from that in which Clayton had been going, started off through the jungle. Clayton followed.

Suddenly Clayton heard a faint gunshot—and then silence.

We must go back a few moments in time to explain that in the cabin by the beach, the two terrified women still clung to each other as they crouched upon a low bench in the gathering darkness. The maid sobbed, while the girl sat dry-eyed and outwardly calm. There came to them the sound of a heavy body brushing against the side of the cabin. A gentle scratching sound was heard on the door.

Moments later, the head of a huge lioness showed in the tiny square of the barred window. Her gleaming eyes were fixed upon them. Then the head disappeared, and for the next twenty minutes the brute sniffed and tore at the door, occasionally giving out a wild cry of rage. At length, however, the lioness abandoned the door, and Jane heard the beast return to the window, where she paused, and then launched herself against the time-worn bars.

The girl heard the wooden rods groan, and a few moments later, on the second attempt, one great paw and the head of the animal thrust within the room. Slowly the powerful neck and shoulders spread the bars apart, and the beast protruded further and further into the room.

Jane drew out the revolver Clayton had left, pointed it at the lioness, and pulled the trigger. There was a flash, a loud crack and an answering roar of pain from the beast. Jane saw the beast fall back from the window, and then she and Esmeralda fainted.

But the lioness was not killed. The bullet had but given her a painful wound in one of her shoulders. In another instant she was back at the window. She saw her prey—the two women—lying senseless upon the floor. Slowly she forced her great bulk, inch by inch, through the window. Now her head was through, now one forepaw and shoulder.

It was on this sight that Jane again opened her eyes.

Meanwhile, Tarzan had heard the strange sounds of the lioness' efforts to force her way through the window, and he swung Clayton up over his shoulders, and began his quick way through the trees, gliding from one vine to the next until they reached the cabin.

The ape-man seized the long tail of the lioness in both hands, and, bracing himself with his feet against the side of the cabin, threw all his mighty strength into the effort to draw the beast out. In a few moments the lioness came tumbling out of the window and onto the ground.

With the quickness of a striking rattlesnake, Tarzan launched himself full upon her back, his strong arms wrapping around the beast. With a shriek, the lioness turned completely over, falling full upon her enemy. Pawing and tearing at the earth and air, she rolled and threw herself this way and that, in an effort to unloose this strange foe.

Higher crept the forearms of the ape-man along her back and around her throat. At last Tarzan snapped the lioness' neck.

In an instant he was on his feet, and for the second time that day Clayton heard the ape-man's savage roar of victory.

In an instant he was on his feet with a roar of victory.

Then he heard Jane's cry:

"Cecil—Mr. Clayton! Oh, what was that?"

Running quickly to the cabin door, Clayton called out that all was safe. She raised the bar on the door, and said, "What was that awful noise?"

"It was the cry of victory from the throat of the man who has just saved your life, Miss Porter. Wait, I will fetch him and you may thank him."

She went with Clayton to the side of the cabin, where lay the dead body of the lioness. Tarzan of the Apes was gone.

Clayton called several times, but there was no reply, and so the two returned to the inside of the cabin. "What a frightful sound!" said Jane.

Then Clayton told her of his experiences with the strange creature—of how the wild man had saved his life. "I cannot make it out at all," he remarked. "At first I thought he might be Tarzan of the Apes, but he neither speaks nor understands English, so he cannot be."

"Well, whatever he may be," said the girl, "we owe him our lives."

Several miles south of the cabin, upon a strip of sandy beach, there stood two old men, arguing. Before them stretched the Atlantic Ocean, at their backs the continent of Africa; close around them loomed the jungle. They had wandered for miles in search of their camp, but always in the wrong direction. They were hopelessly lost.

"Bless me! Professor," said the nearsighted Mr. Philander, "there seems to be someone approaching."

Professor Porter turned and said, "Yes, indeed, though your someone appears to be a lion!"

They speeded up their steps before looking over their shoulders again.

"He is following us!" gasped Mr. Philander. The two old men broke into a dash. From the shadows of the jungle peered two keen eyes, watching this race.

It was Tarzan, of course, and he immediately swung quickly through the vines, drawing first one of the gentlemen up by his collar into a tree, and then the other. The three of them watched from that height until the lion, disgusted with waiting for a meal to drop out of the tree to him, wandered off.

Now for the first time, the professor and Mr. Philander acknowledged Tarzan.

"Good evening, sir!" said the professor.

For reply the man motioned them to follow him, and setting them down upon the jungle floor, set off.

"I think we might continue in his company," said Mr. Philander.

In silence they proceeded for what seemed like hours to the two tired and hopeless old men, but at last they passed over a little rise of ground and were overjoyed to see the cabin lying beneath them, not a hundred yards distant.

Here Tarzan pointed toward the little building and then vanished into the jungle.

"Most remarkable!" gasped the professor, and he and his assistant marched on to the cabin. It was a happy party that found itself once more united. Dawn discovered them still telling of their various adventures, and wondering who the strange hero was.

Esmeralda was positive it was none other than an angel, sent down especially to watch over them.

7. Burials

THE NEWCOMERS' next task was to make the cabin livable, and to this end it was decided to remove the skeletons, although Professor Porter and Mr. Philander were interested in first examining them. The two larger, they said, had belonged to an adult male and female. The smallest skeleton was given but passing attention, as its location, in the crib, left no doubt of its having been the infant of this couple. Even so, Mr. Philander made a startling observation about it, which, however, he refrained from sharing with the others.

As they were preparing the skeleton of the man for burial, Clayton discovered a ring on the man's finger. Examining it, he gave a cry, for the ring bore the crest of Greystoke. At the same time, Jane discovered the books in the cupboard, and on opening to the flyleaf of one of them saw the name *John Clayton, London.*

"Why, Mr. Clayton," she cried, "what does this mean? Here are the names of your relatives in these books!"

"And here," he replied, "is the ring belonging to my uncle, John Clayton, Lord Greystoke."

"But how do you account for these things being here?"

"There is but one way to account for it," said Clayton. "The late Lord Greystoke was not drowned, as was presumed. He died here in this cabin, and this skeleton is all that is left of him."

"Then this must have been poor Lady Greystoke," said Jane.

The bodies of the late Lord and Lady Greystoke were buried beside their little African cabin, and between them was placed the tiny skeleton of the baby of Kala, the ape.

Tarzan watched the ceremony from the trees, but most of all he watched the sweet face and figure of Jane Porter. In his savage soul new emotions were stirring. He could not understand them. He wondered why he felt such great interest in these people—why he had gone to such pains to save the three men. But he did not wonder why he had rescued the girl. She was beautiful!

When the grave was filled with earth, the little party turned back toward the cabin, and Esmeralda, still weeping, chanced to glance toward the harbor.

"Look at those brutes out there!" she cried. "They're deserting us, right here in this jungle!"

And, sure enough, the *Arrow* was making for the open sea, slowly, through the harbor's entrance.

"They promised to leave us guns and ammunition," said Clayton. "The merciless beasts!"

"I regret that they did not visit us before sailing," said Professor Porter. "I had requested them to leave the treasure with us."

Jane looked at her father sadly. "Never mind, daddy," she said. "It is solely for the treasure that the men killed their officers and landed us upon this awful shore."

"Indeed?" wondered the professor, who was all too innocent.

"Yes, sir," confirmed Clayton and Mr. Philander.

Tarzan noted the confusion on the faces of the little group as they witnessed the departure of the *Arrow,* and so, following the course of the ship, he hurried out to the point of land at the north of the harbor's mouth to obtain a nearer view.

Swinging through the trees, he reached the point just as the ship was passing out of the harbor, so that he had an excellent view of this strange, floating house, the like of which he had never seen before. There were some twenty men running here and there about the deck, pulling and hauling on ropes. Suddenly the ship slowed to a crawl, and the anchor was lowered; down came the sails. A few moments later a rowboat was lowered over the side, and in it a large chest was placed. Then a dozen sailors rowed toward the point where Tarzan crouched in the branches of a tree.

In a few minutes, the boat had reached the beach. The men jumped out and lifted the great chest to the sand. They were on the north side of the point, so that their presence was hidden from those at the cabin.

One sailor, pointing at a spot beneath Tarzan's tree, said, "Here's a good place." The soil was soft, and soon they had dug a large hole in which to bury the chest. Then they covered it. Their work done, the sailors returned to the small boat and pulled off rapidly toward the *Arrow*. The ship got under full sail immediately, and bore away toward the southwest.

Tarzan sat wondering about the strange actions of these men, and about the contents of the chest they had buried. He dropped to the ground and began to uncover the earth from atop the chest. When this was done, he dragged the chest from the hole. Four sailors had sweated beneath the burden of its weight—Tarzan of the Apes picked it up as though it had been an empty packing case, and carried it off into the densest part of the jungle.

He could not swing through the trees with it, and so he kept to the trails, and made good time. For several hours he traveled northeast, until he came to the meeting place of the apes. Near the center of the clearing, he began to dig. After much labor he buried the locked chest.

By the time Tarzan had hunted his way back toward the cabin, feeding as he went, it was quite dark.

Within the little building a light was burning, for Clayton had found an unopened tin of oil. The lamps were still usable, and so the interior of the cabin appeared bright as day to the astonished Tarzan. He had often wondered about the purpose of the lamps. As he approached the window nearest the door, he saw that the cabin had been divided into two rooms by a sailcloth. In the front room were the three men, the two older ones deep in conversation, while the youngest read one of Tarzan's books.

Tarzan was not interested in the men, however, so he went to the other window. There was the girl. How beautiful! She was writing at Tarzan's own table beneath the window. Upon a pile of grasses at the far side of the room lay the maid, asleep.

For an hour Tarzan feasted his eyes upon Jane while she wrote. How he longed to speak to her, but he feared that he might frighten her away. Soon she got up, leaving her letter upon the table. She went to the bed, upon which had been spread several layers of soft grasses. Then she loosened her hair, and put out the lamp.

Still Tarzan watched from outside. Cautiously he put his hand through the window to feel upon the desk. At last he grasped the papers upon which Jane had been writing, and pulled them out. He folded the sheets and tucked them into the quiver with his arrows. Then he melted away into the jungle, as softly as a shadow.

Early the next morning Tarzan awoke, and hurriedly brought forth the letter hidden in his quiver. Here is what he read:

TO HAZEL STRONG, BALTIMORE, MARYLAND

West Coast of Africa,
About 10 Degrees South Latitude

February 3, 1909

DEAREST HAZEL:

It seems foolish to write you a letter that you may never see, but I must tell somebody of our awful experiences since we sailed from Europe on the *Arrow.* If we never return to civilization, as now seems likely, this will at least be a brief record of the events which led up to our final fate.

As you know, Papa discovered a long-lost treasure map from 1550, drawn by a Spanish sailor. To make a long story short, we found the treasure—a great iron-bound oak chest. It was simply filled with gold coin, and was so heavy that four men bent beneath its weight. The horrid thing seems to bring nothing but murder and misfortune to those who have anything to do with it, for, three days after we sailed from the Cape Verde Islands, our own crew mutinied and killed every one of their officers.

They were going to kill us, too, but one of them, the leader, would not let them, and so they sailed south along the coast to a lonely spot where they found a good harbor, and there they landed and have left us. They sailed away with the treasure today.

We have had the most extraordinary experiences since we landed here. Papa and Mr. Philander got lost in the jungle, and were chased by a real lion. Mr. Clayton got lost, and was attacked by a wild beast. Esmeralda and I were cornered in an old cabin by a lioness. But the strangest part of it all is the wonder-

The following morning, Jane found her missing letter.

ful creature who rescued us. I have not seen him, but Mr. Clayton and Papa and Mr. Philander have, and they say he is a god-like, dusky-tanned man, with the strength of an elephant and the bravery of a lion. He speaks no English, and vanishes quickly after he has performed some valorous deed.

Then we have another unusual neighbor, who printed a beautiful sign in English and tacked it on the door of his cabin—which we have moved into—warning us to destroy none of his belongings, and signing himself "Tarzan of the Apes." We have never seen him, though we think he is about.

The sailors left us but a meager supply of food, so, as we have only a single revolver with but three bullets left in it, we do not know how we will get meat, though Mr. Philander says we can live on the wild fruit and nuts which abound in this jungle.

I am very tired now, so I shall go to my bed of grasses.

Lovingly,
JANE PORTER

Tarzan sat, after he had finished reading the letter, his brain in a whirl. So they did not know he was Tarzan of the Apes! He would tell them. He had constructed in his tree a rude shelter of leaves and boughs, beneath which, protected from the rain, he kept the few treasures he had brought from the cabin: among these were some pencils.

He took one, and beneath Jane Porter's signature he wrote:

I am Tarzan of the Apes.

He thought that would be enough. Later he would return the letter to the cabin. In the matter of food, thought Tarzan, they had no need to worry—he would provide that.

The following morning, Jane found her missing letter in the exact spot from which it had disappeared two nights before. When she saw the printed words beneath her signature, she felt a chill run up her spine. She showed it to Clayton.

"But he must be friendly," said Clayton, "for he has returned your letter, and he has left the carcass of a wild boar outside the cabin door."

From then on, scarcely a day went by that did not bring its offering of meat. Sometimes it was a young deer, or strange, cooked food—stolen from the Mbonga's village—or a boar, a leopard, and once a lion. Tarzan got great pleasure in hunting for meat for these strangers.

A month passed, and Tarzan finally determined to visit the camp by daylight. It was early afternoon. Clayton had wandered to the point at the harbor's mouth to look for passing ships. Professor Porter was strolling along the beach, with Mr. Philander at his elbow. Jane and Esmeralda had ventured into the jungle to gather fruit.

Tarzan waited in silence before the door of the little cabin for their return. His thoughts were of the beautiful girl; they were always of her now. He wondered if she would fear him. While he waited, he passed the time writing a message to her:

> I am Tarzan of the Apes. I am yours. You are mine. We will live here together always in my house. I will bring you the best fruits, the tenderest deer, the finest meats that the jungle provides. I will hunt for you. I am the greatest of the jungle hunters. I will fight for you. I am the mightiest of the jungle fighters. You are Jane Porter, I saw it in your letter. When you see this you will know that it is for you and that Tarzan of the Apes loves you.

As he stood by the door, waiting after he had finished the message, there came to his keen ears a familiar sound. It was the passing of a great ape through the lower branches of the forest. Then from the jungle came the scream of a woman, and Tarzan, dropping his letter upon the ground, shot like a panther into the forest.

Clayton also heard the scream, as did Professor

Porter and Mr. Philander, and in a few minutes they all arrived at the cabin; Jane and Esmeralda were not there. Instantly, Clayton, followed by the two old men, plunged into the jungle, calling the girl's name aloud. For half an hour they stumbled on, until Clayton came upon the fainted form of Esmeralda.

"Esmeralda," he shouted. "Esmeralda! For God's sake, where is Miss Porter?"

"Isn't Miss Jane here?" cried Esmeralda, sitting up. "Oh, Lord, now I remember! It must have taken her away." And she began to sob.

"What took her away?" said Professor Porter.

"A great big giant all covered with hair."

"A gorilla, Esmeralda?" questioned Mr. Philander.

"I thought it was the devil, but I guess it must have been one of them gorillas. Oh, my poor baby, my poor little honey," and again Esmeralda broke into sobbing.

Clayton began to look about for tracks, but he could find nothing. For the rest of the day they looked for Jane through the jungle, but as night drew on they were forced to give up, for they did not even know in what direction the ape had taken Jane.

It was long after dark before this very sad group reached the cabin.

8. The Call of the Wild

THE NEW KING of the apes, Terkoz, who had taken over when Tarzan left, had been right above Esmeralda and Jane when he first saw them. The first moment Jane became aware of him was when the hairy beast dropped to the earth beside her. One piercing scream escaped her lips as the brute clutched her arm.

This hairless white ape, thought Terkoz, would be one of his wives, and so he threw her across his shoulders and leaped back into the trees, bearing Jane away farther and farther into the jungle.

The scream that had brought Clayton and the two older men stumbling through the undergrowth had led Tarzan straight to where Esmeralda lay, but it was not Esmeralda in whom his interest centered, though he paused over her to see that she was unhurt.

For a moment he studied the ground below and the trees above, until the ape in him, combined with his human intelligence, understood the whole story as plainly as though he had seen the thing happen with his own eyes.

And then he was gone again into the swaying trees, following the trail no other human eye could have noticed. Here, on this branch, a caterpillar had been crushed by the ape's great foot, and Tarzan knew where that same foot would touch in the next stride. Here he looked to find a tiny particle of debris, and there he saw a bit of bark that had been upturned by the scraping hand.

But Tarzan's strongest sense was scent, for his trained nostrils were as sensitive as a hound's. From early infancy his survival had depended on keen eyesight, hearing, smell, touch and taste.

Almost silently the ape-man sped on in the track of Terkoz and Jane, but the sound of his approach reached the ears of the fleeing beast and spurred it on to greater speed. Three miles were covered before Tarzan overtook them, and then Terkoz, seeing that further flight would do him no good, dropped to the ground in a small open glade, that he might turn and fight for his prize, or be free to escape unharmed if he saw that Tarzan was too much for him.

He still grasped Jane in one arm as Tarzan bounded like a leopard into the arena which nature had provided for this battle. From the description which Clayton and her father had given her, Jane knew that the newcomer must be the same wonderful creature who had saved them. But when Terkoz pushed her roughly aside to meet Tarzan's charge, and she saw the size of the ape and its mighty muscles and fierce fangs, she was frightened.

Like two charging bulls the man and beast came together, and like two wolves went for each other's throat. To oppose the long, sharp teeth of the ape was Tarzan's thin-bladed knife.

Jane—backed up against a tree, her hands pressed against her chest, her eyes wide—watched the battle. Before long, Tarzan had stabbed the huge ape a dozen times, and the beast rolled over, dead. Jane then sprang forward with outstretched arms toward the ape-man who had fought for her.

Tarzan took the woman in his arms and kissed her, then swept her up and carried her into the jungle.

Early the following morning, the four within the little cabin by the beach were awakened by the booming of a cannon. Clayton was the first to rush out, and there, beyond the harbor's mouth, he saw two ships lying at anchor.

One was the *Arrow,* the ship which had abandoned them there, and the other a small French cruiser. The sides of the French ship were crowded with men gazing shoreward. Both vessels lay at a great distance from shore, and it was doubtful whether they could see the waving hats of the little group. Esmeralda removed her red apron and waved it frantically above her head, and Clayton hurried off toward the northern point where lay his pile of wood, heaped up for just this occasion. Quickly lighting the pile in a dozen places, he hurried to the point of the land, where he stripped off his shirt, and, tying it to a branch, stood waving it back and forth above him.

Soon Clayton saw the two ships begin to steam slowly back toward shore. At some distance away they stopped, and a boat was lowered and rowed toward the beach. As it drew up onto the sand, a young French officer stepped out.

"Monsieur Clayton, I presume?" he asked.

"Thank God, you have come!" was Clayton's reply. "And it may be that it is not too late, even now."

"What do you mean?"

Clayton then told of how the ape had stolen away Jane Porter.

"Mon Dieu!" exclaimed the officer.

Soon the entire party had come ashore, where stood Professor Porter, Mr. Philander and the weeping

Esmeralda waved her apron frantically above her head.

Esmeralda. Among the officers in the last of the boats to put off from the French ship was the commander, and when he had heard the story of Jane's kidnapping, he called for volunteers to go with Professor Porter and Clayton in their search.

Not an officer or a man was there who did not quickly volunteer. The commander then selected twenty men and two officers, Lieutenant D'Arnot and Lieutenant Charpentier. Within a few minutes the group of sailors and the two French officers, together with Professor Porter and Clayton, set off upon their quest into the jungle.

When Jane realized she was being carried away a captive by the strange forest creature who had rescued her, she lay quietly in his strong arms, looking through half-closed eyes at the face of this man who strode so easily through the tangled undergrowth with her. He seemed to her extraordinarily beautiful.

Soon Tarzan took to the trees, and Jane, wondering that she felt no fear, began to realize that she had never felt more safe in her life than now, lying in the arms of this strong, wild creature, being carried, God alone knew where, deeper and deeper into the savage jungle.

When they had come to their destination, Tarzan of the Apes, with Jane in his grasp, swung lightly to the turf of the open space where the great apes held their meetings.

Though they had come many miles, it was still but midafternoon. The green turf looked soft and cool. The many noises of the jungle seemed far away and hushed, like surf upon a distant shore. A feeling of dreaminess stole over Jane as she sank down upon the grass where Tarzan had placed her. As she watched him, Tarzan crossed the clearing toward the trees upon the further side. She thought what a perfect creature he looked! Never had such a man walked the earth since God created Adam.

With a bound Tarzan sprang into the trees and disappeared. Jane wondered where he had gone. Had he left her there to her fate in the lonely jungle? She glanced nervously about. Every vine and bush seemed to be the lurking place of some huge and horrible beast. Every sound terrified her.

For a few minutes, which seemed hours to the frightened girl, she sat with tense nerves. She heard a sudden, slight sound behind her. With a shriek she sprang to her feet and turned to face her end. Instead, there stood Tarzan, his arms filled with ripe fruit.

Jane became dizzy and would have fallen, had not Tarzan, dropping the fruit, caught her in his arms. Tarzan stroked her soft hair, and tried to comfort and quiet her as Kala had him, when, as a little ape, he had been frightened by Sabor, the lioness, or Histah, the snake. He pressed his lips upon her forehead, and she sighed.

Then she pointed to the fruit upon the ground, and seated herself, for she was hungry. Tarzan quickly gathered up the fruit, and, bringing it, laid it at her feet; then he, too, sat, and with his knife prepared the fruits for her meal. Together and in silence they ate, until finally Jane said, "I wish you spoke English."

Tarzan shook his head. Then Jane tried speaking to him in French and in German. Again Tarzan shook his head.

Finally, he got up and went into the trees, though not without first trying to explain, by signs, that he would return shortly; he signaled so well that Jane understood and was not afraid when he had gone. Only a feeling of loneliness came over her, and she watched with longing eyes the point where he had disappeared, awaiting his return. As before, she knew he had returned when she heard a soft sound behind her, and she turned to see him coming across the turf with an armful of branches.

He then went back again into the jungle, and in a few minutes he reappeared, his arms filled with soft grasses and ferns. Two more trips he made, until he had gathered quite a pile of material. Then he spread the ferns and grasses upon the ground in a soft flat bed, and above it he leaned many branches together so that they met a few feet over its center. Upon these he spread layers of huge leaves, and with more branches and more leaves he closed one end of the little shelter he had built.

Then they sat down together and tried to talk by signs. The magnificent diamond locket which hung about Tarzan's neck had been a source of much wonder to Jane. She pointed to it now, and Tarzan removed it and handed it to her.

She noticed that the locket opened, and, pressing the hidden clasp, she saw the two halves spring apart to reveal in either section a miniature portrait. One was of a beautiful woman, and the other might have been a likeness of the man who sat beside her. She looked up at Tarzan to find him leaning toward her, gazing on the miniatures with astonishment. His manner showed her that he had never before seen them, nor even guessed that the locket opened. Jane now wondered how this necklace had come to a wild and savage creature of the jungle. She also wondered how it could be that the image of the man in the locket resembled this forest god.

Tarzan gazed at the two faces for a moment. Soon he removed the quiver of arrows from his shoulder, and, emptying its contents upon the ground, he reached into the bottom of the quiver and drew out a flat object wrapped in many soft leaves and tied with bits of long grass. Carefully he unwrapped it, removing layer after layer of leaves, until at length he held a photograph in his hand.

Pointing to the miniature of the man within the locket, he handed the photograph to Jane, holding the open locket beside it. The photograph only served to puzzle the girl still more, for it was evidently another likeness of the same man whose picture rested in the locket beside that of the beautiful young woman.

Jane pointed to the photograph and then to the miniature and then to him, as though to show that she thought the likenesses were of him, but he only shook his head, and then, shrugging his shoulders, he took the photograph from her and rewrapped it before placing it again in the bottom of his quiver.

Jane held the little locket in her hand, turning it over and over until a simple explanation occurred to her. The locket had belonged to Lord Greystoke, and the likenesses were of himself and Lady Alice. This wild creature had simply found it in the cabin by the beach. How stupid of her not to have thought of that before. But to account for the likeness between Lord Greystoke and this forest god—that was quite beyond her, and it is not strange that she did not imagine that this half-naked savage was indeed an English nobleman.

It was growing dark now, and so they ate again of the fruit which was both food and drink for them, and then Tarzan rose and leading Jane to the little bower he had built, motioned her to go within.

The girl entered and lay down upon the soft grasses, while Tarzan of the Apes stretched himself upon the ground across the entrance.

When Jane awoke, she did not at first recall the strange events of the day before, and so she wondered at her odd surroundings—the little leafy bower, the soft grasses of her bed, the unusual view from the opening at her feet. After she remembered why she was there, she moved to the entrance of the shelter to look for Tarzan. He was gone; but this time she was not frightened, for she knew that he would return.

In the grass at the entrance to her bower she saw the

imprint of his body where he had lain all night to guard her. With him near, who could be afraid? She wondered if there was any other man on earth with whom a girl could feel so safe in the middle of this jungle. Why, even the lions no longer scared her now! She looked up to see him drop softly from a nearby tree. As he caught her eyes upon him, his face lit up with a bright smile.

He had again been gathering fruit, and this he laid at the entrance of her bower. Once more they sat down together to eat. When they had finished their breakfast, Tarzan motioned to her to follow. He walked toward the trees at the edge of the clearing, and took her in one strong arm and swung to the branches above.

The girl knew that he was taking her back to her people, so she could not understand the sudden feeling of sorrow which crept over her.

For hours they swung slowly along. Tarzan did not hurry. Several times they halted for a brief rest, which he did not need, and at noon they stopped for an hour at a little stream, where they quenched their thirst and ate. It was nearly sunset when they came to the cabin, and Tarzan, dropping to the ground beside a great tree, parted the tall jungle grass and pointed out the little cabin to her. She took him by the hand to lead him to it, that she might tell her father that this man had saved her from death, and that he had watched over her as carefully as a mother might have done. But Tarzan drew back, shaking his head.

The girl came close to him, looking up with pleading eyes. Somehow she could not bear the thought of his going back into the jungle alone. Still he shook his head, and finally he drew her to him very gently and stooped to kiss her. She threw her arms around his neck and kissed him back.

"I love you," she said. "I love you."

From far in the distance came the faint sound of many guns. Tarzan and Jane stopped and listened; the noise brought Esmeralda and Mr. Philander out of the cabin as well. From where Tarzan and the girl stood, they could not see the two ships lying at anchor in the harbor. Tarzan pointed toward the sounds, touched his chest, and pointed again. She understood. He was going, and something told her that it was because he thought her people were in danger.

"Come back to me," she whispered. "I shall wait for you—always."

Then he was gone—and Jane turned to walk across the clearing to the cabin.

Mr. Philander was the first to see her. "Jane!" he cried. "Jane Porter! Bless me! Where did you come from? Where in the world have you been? How—"

"Mercy, Mr. Philander," interrupted the girl. "I never can remember so many questions."

"Well, well," said Mr. Philander. "Bless me! I am so filled with surprise and delight at seeing you safe and well again that I scarcely know what I am saying, really. But come, tell me all that has happened to you."

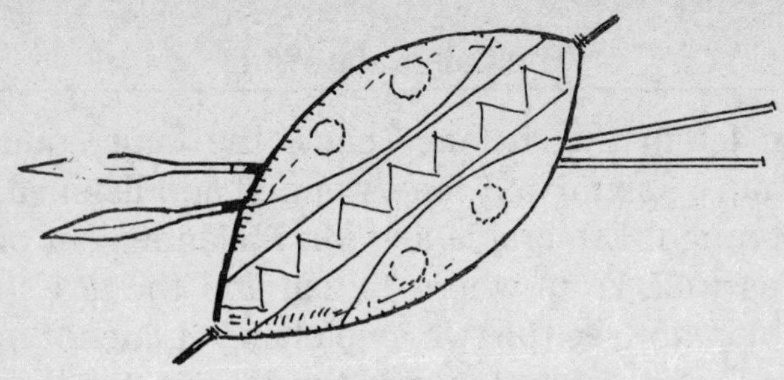

9. French Lessons

As the little expedition of sailors toiled through the dense jungle, searching for signs of Jane Porter, the hopelessness of their venture became more and more clear, but the grief of the old man and the heart-sick eyes of the young Englishman prevented the kind-hearted D'Arnot from turning back. He sent out his men in formation from where Esmeralda had been found, and they sweated their way through the tangled vines.

It was slow work. Noon found them but a few miles inland. They halted for a brief rest then, and after pushing on for a short distance, one of the men discovered a well marked trail. It was an old elephant track, and D'Arnot decided that they all should follow it. He was in the lead and moving at a quick pace when a half dozen tribal warriors suddenly arose about him.

D'Arnot gave a warning shout to his men as the warriors closed in on him, but before he could draw his revolver he found himself gripped by his arms and dragged into the jungle.

His cry had alarmed the sailors, and a dozen of them ran up the trail to their officer's aid. A spear struck one man, and then a volley of arrows fell among them. Raising their rifles, they fired into the underbrush in the direction from which the arrows had come. It was these shots that Tarzan and Jane had heard.

Lieutenant Charpentier, who had been bringing up the rear of the line of men, now came running to the scene, and, on hearing the details of the ambush, he ordered the men to follow him. In an instant they were in a hand-to-hand fight with some fifty warriors of Mbonga's village. Arrows and bullets flew thick and fast.

Minutes later, the warriors backtracked, but the Frenchmen did not follow, as four of their twenty were dead, a dozen others were wounded and Lieutenant D'Arnot was missing. Night was falling, and so they made camp where they were.

The warriors who seized D'Arnot had in the meantime hurried him along, and they now brought him to a good-sized clearing, at one end of which stood their thatched and gated village. It was now dusk, but the gatekeepers saw the approaching prisoner, and a cry went up. A great throng of women and children rushed out to meet the group.

Then began for the French officer the most terrifying experience a man can encounter upon earth—the reception of a prisoner into a village of cannibals.

They fell upon D'Arnot tooth and nail, beating him with sticks and stones and tearing at him, but not once did the Frenchman cry out in pain. They soon arrived at the center of the village, where D'Arnot was tied up to a post from which no live man had ever been released. A number of women scattered to their several huts to fetch pots and water, while others built a row of fires on which portions of the feast were to be boiled.

Half fainting from pain, D'Arnot watched what seemed to be a nightmare.

Tarzan of the Apes knew what those sounds had meant. With Jane's kisses still warm upon his lips, he swung with incredible swiftness through the forest, straight toward Mbonga's village. He was not interested in the location of the battle, for he judged that that would soon be over. Those who were killed he could not help; those who escaped would not need his help. It was to those who had neither been killed nor had escaped that he hurried. And he knew that he would find them by the post in Mbonga's village.

Many times had Tarzan seen Mbonga's raiding parties return from the north with prisoners, and always were the same scenes carried out about that stake, beneath the light of many fires.

He knew, too, that the villagers seldom lost much time before eating their captives. On he sped. Night had fallen and he traveled high along the trees, where the tropic moon lighted the confusing pathway through the gently waving treetops. In a few minutes Tarzan swung into the trees above Mbonga's village. Ah, he was not too late! Or was he? He could not tell. The figure at the stake was very still, yet the warriors continued to prick it with their spears.

Tarzan knew their customs. The death blow had not been struck. The stake stood forty feet from the nearest tree. Tarzan coiled his rope. Then there rose suddenly above the singing of the villagers Tarzan's terrible, apelike cry.

The dancers halted as though turned to stone.

Tarzan flung the rope high above the villagers. It was unseen in the flaring lights of the campfires.

D'Arnot opened his eyes. A huge tribesman, standing directly before him, lunged backward as though struck by an invisible hand. Struggling and shrieking, the tribesman, rolling from side to side, was jerked quickly toward the shadows beneath the trees. Once beneath the trees, the body rose straight into the air, and as it disappeared into the leaves above, the terrified vil-

The figure at the stake was very still.

lagers, screaming with fright, broke into a mad race for the gates.

D'Arnot was left alone. As he watched the spot where the body had entered the tree, he heard the sounds of movement there. The branches swayed—there was a crash and the warrior came sprawling to earth again.

Immediately after him came a young giant, who moved quickly toward him from the shadows into the firelight. What could it mean? Who could it be?

Without a word Tarzan of the Apes cut the bonds which held the Frenchman. Weak from suffering and loss of blood, D'Arnot would have fallen but for the strong arms that caught him.

The French officer felt himself lifted from the ground. There was a sensation as of flying, and then he fainted.

It was not until late the next afternoon that the patrol reached the clearing by the beach. For Professor Porter and Cecil Clayton, the return brought such great happiness that all their sufferings were forgotten. As the little party emerged from the jungle, the first person that the professor and Clayton saw was Jane, standing by the cabin door.

With a little cry of joy she ran forward to greet them, throwing her arms around her father's neck and bursting into tears. Professor Porter sobbed as well. Clayton's heart was filled with happiness to see that the woman he loved was safe. "Jane!" he cried. "God has been good to us, indeed. Tell me how you escaped."

"Mr. Clayton," she said, offering her hand to shake, "let me thank you for your loyalty to my father. He told me how good you were to accompany him in his search for me. How can we ever repay you?"

"I am already repaid," he said, "just to see you and the professor both safe, well and together again."

"But tell me," said Jane, "where is the forest man who went to rescue you? Why did he not return?"

"I do not understand," said Clayton. "Whom do you mean?"

"He who has saved each of us—who saved me from the gorilla."

"Oh?" said Clayton in surprise. "It was he who rescued you? You have not told me anything of your adventure. Please tell me."

"But, no—haven't you seen him? When we heard the shots in the jungle, he left me. We had just reached the clearing, and he hurried off in the direction of the shots. I know he went to help you."

"We did not see him," said Clayton. "He did not join us. Possibly he joined his own tribe—the men who attacked us."

"No!" said Jane. "It could not be. They were savages—he is a gentleman."

Clayton looked puzzled, and remarked of the man he did not know was his cousin, "He is a strange, half-savage creature of the jungle, Miss Porter. We know nothing of him. He neither speaks nor understands any European language—and his jewelry and weapons are those of the savages." He saw she was made unhappy by these words, but he continued. "There are no other human beings than savages within hundreds of miles. He must belong to the tribes which attacked us—he may even be a cannibal, a man-eater."

"No, I will not believe it," said Jane. "It's not true. You do not know him as I do."

"Possibly you are right, Jane," said Clayton, "but the chances are that he is some half-crazed castaway who will forget us quickly. He is only a beast of the jungle."

The girl did not answer. Slowly she turned and walked back to the cabin, murmuring to herself, "Beast? Then God make me a beast; for, man or beast, I am his!"

The next morning Clayton left early with the expedition in search of Lieutenant D'Arnot, for they did not know that Tarzan had already rescued the officer.

When D'Arnot came out of his faint, he found himself lying upon a bed of soft ferns and grasses beneath a little A-shaped shelter of boughs. At his feet, an opening

D'Arnot tried to talk with the man, but it was useless.

looked out upon a green clearing, and at a little distance beyond was a wall of jungle. He was very lame and sore and weak.

After some time he remembered the whole terrifying scene at the stake of the natives, and he finally recalled the strange figure in whose arms he had fainted away. He wondered what would happen now. He could not see or hear any signs of life. The hum of the jungle—the rustling of millions of leaves—the buzz of insects—the voices of birds and monkeys—seemed blended into a purr. Suddenly, through the opening at his feet, he saw the figure of Tarzan.

The ape-man came toward the shelter. Stooping, he crawled into the shelter beside the wounded officer, and placed a cool hand upon his forehead.

D'Arnot spoke to him in French, but the man only shook his head. Then D'Arnot tried English, but still the man shook his head. Then he tried Italian, Spanish and German, but with the same response from Tarzan.

After he had examined D'Arnot's wounds, Tarzan left the shelter and disappeared. In half an hour he was back with fruit and a hollow gourd filled with water. D'Arnot drank and ate a little. Again he tried to talk with the strange man, but it was useless.

Suddenly Tarzan hurried from the shelter, only to return a few minutes later with several pieces of bark and—wonder of wonders—a lead pencil. Squatting beside D'Arnot, Tarzan wrote for a minute on the smooth inner surface of the bark, then handed it to the Frenchman. D'Arnot was astonished to see, in plain print, a message in English:

"I am Tarzan of the Apes. Who are you? Can you read this language?"

"Yes!" cried out D'Arnot, "I read English. I speak it also. Now we may talk. First let me thank you for all that you have done."

The man only shook his head and pointed to the pencil.

"Mon Dieu!" cried D'Arnot. "If you are English, why is it then that you cannot speak English? You must be a deaf mute!" So he wrote to Tarzan a message on the bark, in English:

"I am Paul D'Arnot, lieutenant in the navy of France. I thank you for what you have done for me. You have saved my life, and all that I have is yours. May I ask how it is that one who writes in English does not speak it?"

Tarzan's neatly printed reply filled D'Arnot with wonder:

"I speak only the language of my tribe—the great apes who were Kerchak's, and a little of the languages of Tantor, the elephant, and Numa, the lion. With a human being I have never spoken, except once with Jane, by signs. This is the first time I have spoken with another of my kind through written words."

D'Arnot was amazed. It seemed incredible that there lived upon earth a full-grown man who had never spoken with a fellow man. He looked again at Tarzan's message, and wrote, "Where is Jane?"

And Tarzan replied: "Back with her people in the cabin of Tarzan of the Apes."

"She is not dead then?" wrote D'Arnot. "What happened to her?"

Tarzan took the pencil now and wrote: "She is not dead. She was taken by Terkoz to be his wife, but Tarzan took her away from Terkoz and killed him before he could harm her. None in all the jungle may face Tarzan of the Apes in battle, and live."

For many days D'Arnot lay upon his bed of soft ferns. The second day a fever had come and D'Arnot thought that it meant he would die. An idea came to him. He called Tarzan and wrote to him: "Can you go to my people and lead them here? I will write a message that you may take to them, and they will follow you."

Tarzan shook his head and wrote: "I had thought of that the first day, but I dared not. The great apes come often to this spot, and if they found you here, wounded and alone, they would kill you."

D'Arnot lay in a fever for three more days, and Tarzan

sat beside him, and bathed his head and hands and washed his wounds. Two days after the fever had passed, D'Arnot was able to stand with Tarzan's help, but he was still as weak as a baby.

D'Arnot wrote his rescuer a message: "What can I do to repay you for all that you have done for me?"

"Teach me to speak the language of men," wrote Tarzan.

And so D'Arnot began at once, pointing out the familiar objects and repeating their names in French, for he thought it would be easier to teach this man his own language.

So when Tarzan pointed to the word *man* which he had printed upon a piece of bark, he learned from D'Arnot that it was pronounced "homme," and in the same way he was taught to pronounce *ape* as "singe" and *tree* as "arbre."

He was an eager student, and in two more days he had mastered so much French that he could speak little sentences such as: "That is a tree"; "This is grass"; "I am hungry." The Frenchman wrote little lessons for Tarzan in English, and had Tarzan repeat them in French, but this was often confusing for them both. D'Arnot realized now he had made a mistake of crossing the languages, but it seemed too late to go back and do it all over again.

On the third day of lessons Tarzan wrote D'Arnot a message asking if he felt strong enough to be carried back to the cabin.

"But you cannot carry me all the distance through this jungle," wrote D'Arnot.

"Mais oui!" Tarzan said, and D'Arnot laughed aloud to hear the phrase from the ape-man's mouth.

So they set out, D'Arnot marveling as had Clayton and Jane at the wondrous strength of the ape-man.

Midafternoon brought them to the clearing.

Midafternoon brought them to the clearing, and as Tarzan dropped to earth from the branches of the last tree, his heart leaped in expectation of seeing Jane. But no one was in sight near the cabin, and D'Arnot was surprised to notice that the two ships were no longer at anchor in the bay outside the harbor.

Neither spoke, but both knew before they opened the closed cabin door what they would find within. Tarzan lifted the latch and pushed open the door. It was as they feared; the cabin was deserted. The men turned and looked at one another.

D'Arnot knew that his men thought him dead, but

Tarzan thought only of the woman who had kissed him and now had fled from him. But as Tarzan stood in the doorway brooding, D'Arnot noticed that many supplies had been left from the ship: a camping stove, some forks and knives, a rifle and ammunition, canned foods, blankets, two chairs and a cot.

"They must intend to return," said D'Arnot. He walked over to the table that John Clayton had built so many years before to serve as a desk, and on it he saw two notes addressed to Tarzan. He handed them to the ape-man, and Tarzan sat down on a stool and read them.

> To Tarzan of the Apes:
>
> We thank you for the use of your cabin, and are sorry that we could not thank you in person. We have harmed nothing of your goods, but have left many things for you which may add to your comfort. If you know the strange jungle-man who saved our lives and brought us food, thank him for his kindness.
>
> We sail in an hour, never to return.
>
> Very gratefully,
> CECIL CLAYTON

Tarzan had a look of sorrow as he read through this letter, which he then handed to D'Arnot. The second, as Tarzan feared, was from Jane:

> To Tarzan of the Apes:
>
> Before I leave, let me add my thanks to those of Mr. Clayton for the kindness you have shown in permitting us the use of your cabin. That you never came to make friends with us has been a regret to us.
>
> There is another I should like to thank also, but he did not come back, though I cannot believe that he is dead. I do not know his name. He is the great giant

who wore the diamond locket upon his chest. If you know him and can speak his language, carry my thanks to him, and tell him that I waited seven days for him to return.

Tell him, also, that in my home in America, in the city of Baltimore, there will always be a welcome for him.

I found a note you wrote me lying among the leaves beneath a tree near the cabin. I do not know how you learned to love me, but I must tell you that I already love another.

I shall always be your friend,
JANE PORTER

It was evident to him from the notes that they did not know that he and Tarzan of the Apes were one and the same. *"I already love another!"* he sighed to himself again and again. Then she did not love *him!* How could she have pretended to love him? Maybe her kisses were only signs of friendship. How was he to know, who knew nothing of the customs of human beings?

Suddenly, he turned to D'Arnot and asked, "Where is America?"

D'Arnot pointed toward the northwest, and said, "Many thousands of miles across the ocean. Why?"

"I am going there."

D'Arnot shook his head. "It is impossible, my friend." D'Arnot pulled an atlas from the bookshelf, showing the ape-man that the blue represented all the water on the earth, and the bits of other colors the continents and islands. Tarzan asked him to point out the spot where they now were.

D'Arnot did so.

"Now point out America," said Tarzan.

And as D'Arnot placed his finger upon North America, Tarzan smiled and laid his palm upon the page, spanning the great ocean that lay between Africa and the Americas.

"You see, it is not so very far," said Tarzan.

D'Arnot laughed. Then he took a pencil and made a tiny point upon the shore of Africa. "This little mark is many times larger upon this map than your cabin is upon the earth. Do you see now how very far it is?"

Tarzan thought for a long time. "Do any Frenchmen live in Africa?"

"Yes."

"And where are the nearest?"

D'Arnot pointed out a spot on the shore just north of them.

"Have they big boats to cross the ocean?" asked Tarzan.

"Yes."

"We shall go there tomorrow," announced Tarzan.

So on the following day they started north along the shore. For a month they traveled north, sometimes finding food in plenty, and again going hungry for days.

Tarzan asked questions and learned rapidly. D'Arnot taught him many of the refinements of civilization—even the use of knife and fork.

On the journey Tarzan told D'Arnot about the great chest he had dug up and carried to the gathering place of the apes, where it now lay buried.

"It must be the treasure chest of Professor Porter!" exclaimed D'Arnot. Then Tarzan remembered the letter written by Jane to her friend—the one he had stolen when they first came to his cabin, and now he knew what was in the chest and what it meant to Jane.

"Tomorrow we shall go back after it," he announced to D'Arnot.

"Go back?" wondered D'Arnot. "But, my dear fellow, we have now been three weeks upon the march. It

For a month they traveled north.

would require three more to return to the treasure, and then, with that enormous weight, it would be months before we made it this far again. I have a better plan, my friend. We shall go on together to the nearest settlement, and there we will charter a boat and sail back down the coast for the treasure, and so transport it easily."

"Very well," said Tarzan.

At last they reached the settlement. For a week they remained there, and the ape-man, keenly observant, learned much of the ways of men. Tarzan saw many boats, and gradually he became used to the strange noises and odd ways of civilization. D'Arnot purchased clothes for him, and so no one knew that this handsome young Frenchman had been, only weeks before, swinging half-naked through the jungle.

D'Arnot succeeded in chartering an old boat for the coastal trip to Tarzan's harbor. The trip was uneventful, and the morning after they dropped anchor before the cabin, Tarzan, once more dressed in his jungle costume, set out for the meeting place of the apes. Late the next day he returned, bearing the great chest upon his shoulder, and at sunrise the little boat made its northward journey.

Three weeks later Tarzan and D'Arnot were on board a French steamer bound for Marseilles, and after a few days in that city D'Arnot took Tarzan to Paris. During the journey, Tarzan showed his friend the diary which John Clayton, Lord Greystoke, had written in French, and which the ape-man had carried as a keepsake within his quiver of arrows; once he had read the journal, D'Arnot was almost able to convince his friend that his mother had been not Kala, the kind ape, but Lady Alice, and that he, Tarzan, was rightfully the new Lord Greystoke.

"Then how is it that a baby's skeleton was found within the cabin, mon ami?" asked Tarzan. "Was that not the child of the Greystokes?"

"I do not know how to account for the skeleton, Tarzan, but as sure as I am D'Arnot, I am sure you are Greystoke."

10. Tarzan to the Rescue

UPON THEIR return to America, Jane Porter, her father, Mr. Philander, Esmeralda and Clayton visited the little farm Jane's mother had left her in Wisconsin. Jane had not been there since childhood.

The farmhouse stood on a little hill. It had been filled recently with every modern convenience—a gift from Clayton. Jane understood that Clayton loved her and wished her to be his bride.

"You know we can't repay you," cried Jane. "Why do you want me to be under such obligations?"

"It's not just for you, Jane," said Clayton. "It's for your dear old father. I could not bear to see him staying in the place as I and Philander found it."

"Oh, Cecil, then I thank you."

The next morning found a cloud of smoke lying low over the nearby forest, but it was not seen by the visitors to the farm, and Jane did not notice it as she set off unaccompanied on a walk. She would not let her admirer Clayton go with her; she wanted to be alone, she said, and he respected her wishes.

As Jane walked, Professor Porter and Mr. Philander remained in the house, discussing a weighty scientific problem. Esmeralda dozed in the kitchen and Clayton lay napping on the couch in the living room.

To the east, black smoke clouds rose high into the heavens, and then began to blow west. On and on the black clouds came, the wind carrying the forest fire in the direction in which Jane was walking. For many minutes she did not notice the smoke, for it blew along the treetops.

A French automobile approached the house Jane had left, coming from the northeast. With a jolt it stopped in front of the cottage, and a black-haired giant leaped out to run up onto the porch. Without a pause he rushed into the house. On the couch lay Clayton. The newcomer was at the side of the sleeping man with a bound. Shaking him roughly by the shoulder, he cried: "My God, Clayton, are you all crazy? Don't you know a fire is nearing? Where is Miss Jane Porter?"

Clayton sprang to his feet. He did not recognize the man, but he understood the words and was up and outside on the veranda in a moment. "Great Scott!" he cried, and then, dashing back into the house, "Jane! Jane! Where are you?"

"She's gone for a walk," said Esmeralda.

"Which way did she go?" demanded the black-haired man of Esmeralda.

"Down that road," cried the frightened maid, pointing to where a wall of roaring flames shut out the view.

The muscular figure sprinted away across the clearing toward the fire.

"Who *was* that?" asked Professor Porter.

"I do not know," replied Clayton. "He called me by name and knew Jane, for he asked for her. And he called Esmeralda by name."

"There was something familiar about him," exclaimed Mr. Philander, "and yet I know I never saw him before."

When Jane had turned to retrace her steps homeward, she was alarmed to note how near the smoke of the forest fire seemed, and she hurried onward. A short run down the road brought her to a halt, for there before her was another wall of flame. She realized it would be but a matter of minutes before she was met by fire on all sides.

Suddenly she heard her name being called aloud through the forest:

"Jane! Jane Porter!" It rang strong and clear, but in an unfamiliar voice.

"Here!" she called in reply. "Here! In the roadway!"

They had passed beyond the fire now.

Then through the branches of the trees she saw a figure swinging with the speed of a squirrel. The wind blew a cloud of smoke about them, and she could no longer see the man who was speeding toward her, but suddenly she felt an arm around her. Then she was lifted up, and she felt the rushing of the wind as she was carried along.

She opened her eyes. Far below her lay the undergrowth and the hard earth. About her were the waving branches and leaves of the forest. From tree to tree swung the giant figure who carried her, and it seemed to Jane that she was living over in a dream the time she had spent in the African jungle. And, of course, it was the same man who was carrying her!

"My jungle-man!" she said.

"Yes," smiled Tarzan, "your jungle-man, Jane; I am that savage who has come out of his jungle to claim his mate—the woman who ran away from him."

"I did not run away," said Jane. "We waited a week for you to return, and they would not allow me to stay."

They had passed beyond the fire now, and they now returned to earth. Side by side they began walking toward the cottage. The wind had changed once more and the fire was burning back upon itself—another hour and it would be burned out.

"Why did you not return?" she asked.

"I was nursing D'Arnot. He was badly wounded."

"I knew it!" she cried. "They said you had gone to join the savage tribe—that they were your people."

He laughed. "But you did not believe them, Jane?"

"No!" She smiled. "What shall I call you?"

"I was Tarzan of the Apes when you first knew me," he said.

"Tarzan!" she exclaimed. "Then that was your note! I was sure it wasn't yours, for Tarzan of the Apes had written to us in English, and you could not understand a word of it."

Tarzan laughed. "It is a long story, but it was I who wrote what I could not speak—and now D'Arnot has made matters worse by teaching me to speak French instead of English. But these words I do know: Jane Porter, will you marry me?"

She did not reply. What did she know of this strange creature? What did he know of himself? Who was he? Who were his parents? Why, his very name showed his strange and savage life. Could she be happy with this jungle orphan? Could she find anything in common with a husband whose life had been spent in the treetops of a jungle, frolicking and fighting with fierce apes, tearing his food from fresh-killed prey, while his fellows growled and fought for their share?

"You do not answer," he said.

"I do not know what answer to make," said Jane.

"You do not love me?"

"Don't ask me that—not that. You will be happier without me. You were never meant for civilization, and in a little while you would miss the freedom of your old life."

"I see now that you could not be happy with—an ape."

"Don't say that," said Jane. "You don't understand."

She remembered the spell that had been upon her in the depths of that far-off jungle, but there was no spell of enchantment now in Wisconsin. Did she love him? She did not know—now.

She thought of Clayton. Did not her best judgment point to this young English nobleman, whose love she knew to be of the sort a woman should want? Could she love Clayton? She could see no reason why she could not.

Before long they were with her father and friends. At the sight of Jane, cries of relief and delight came from all, and Professor Porter took his daughter in his arms.

Clayton held out his hand to Tarzan. "How can we ever thank you? You have saved Jane.—You called me by name in the cottage, but I do not seem to remember yours, though there is something very familiar about you."

Tarzan smiled and he took Clayton's hand. "You are quite right, Monsieur Clayton," he said, in French. "You will pardon me if I do not speak to you in English. I am just learning it, and while I understand it fairly well, I speak it very poorly."

"But who are you?"

"Tarzan of the Apes."

"By Jove!" Clayton exclaimed. "It is true!"

And Professor Porter and Mr. Philander came forward now to express their thanks to Tarzan, and to voice their surprise and pleasure at seeing their jungle friend so far from his savage home.

Tarzan, on his part, was pleased to say to Jane's father: "Your treasure has been found."

"What—what is that you are saying? It cannot be."

"It is, though. I saw the sailors bury it, and, ape-like, I had to dig it up and bury it again elsewhere. When D'Arnot told me what it was—and what it meant to you—I returned to the jungle and recovered it. Mr. D'Arnot is holding it for you."

"To the already tremendous thanks we owe you, sir," said Professor Porter, "we now add more."

"Bless me!" exclaimed Mr. Philander. "Who would ever have thought it possible! The last time we saw you you were a wild-man, leaping about among the branches of a jungle, and now you are in Wisconsin, having arrived in a French automobile! It is remarkable."

"Yes," agreed Tarzan, asking then for a private word with the man. "Mr. Philander, do you recall any of the details of the finding and burying of three skeletons found in my jungle cabin?"

"I remember everything," said Mr. Philander.

"I want you to answer my question to the best of your knowledge—were the three skeletons you buried all human skeletons?"

"No," said Mr. Philander, "the smallest one, the one found in the crib, was the skeleton of an ape."

"Thank you," said Tarzan. He now knew with certainty that he was the son of Lord and Lady Greystoke, rather than that of Kala and a white-skinned ape.

As the two men talked, Clayton took Jane off to one side, out of hearing of Tarzan. The English lord asked, "Won't you say yes to my proposal now, Jane? I will devote my life to making you very happy."

"Yes," she whispered.

That evening, in the cottage, Tarzan found the chance to be alone with Jane. He said, "For your sake I have become a civilized man—for your sake I have crossed oceans and continents—for your sake I will be whatever you want me to be. I can make you happy, Jane, in the life you know and love best. Will you marry me?"

For the first time Jane realized the depths of the man's love—all that he had done in so short a time solely out of love for her. Turning her head, she sobbed. What had she done? Because she had been afraid she might agree to Tarzan's proposal she had accepted Clayton's. She confessed this to the jungle-man.

"What can we do?" he asked. "You have admitted that you love me. You know that I love you. But I do not

"I could never face you if I broke my promise to Mr. Clayton."

know the rules of your society. I shall leave the decision to you."

"I cannot tell Clayton now, Tarzan," she said. "He, too, loves me, and he is a good man. I could never face you nor any other honest person if I broke my promise to Mr. Clayton."

Tarzan turned his face away. By Mr. Philander's confirmation, Tarzan now knew that he—not Clayton—was in fact the rightful Lord Greystoke, and yet Clayton was going to marry the woman whom Tarzan loved—the woman who loved Tarzan. If Tarzan told them who he truly was, what a great difference it would make! It would take away Clayton's title and land and his castles, and—it would take them away from Jane also.

The happy Clayton approached the silent Tarzan and Jane. "I say, old man," said Clayton, patting the jungleman on the shoulder. "I haven't had a chance to thank you for all you've done for us. It seems as though you've had your hands full, saving our lives in Africa and here. I'm awfully glad you came on here. I often thought about you, you know, and the amazing life you led. If it's any of my business, how the devil did you ever get into that jungle?"

Tarzan replied, "I was born there, and my mother was an ape. I never knew who my father was." For Jane's sake, Tarzan had renounced his title of Lord Greystoke.